Oscar

Oscar and Grace

The Davenports

Book One

SJ McCoy

A Sweet n Steamy Romance

Published by Xenion, Inc

Published by Xenion, Inc.
First Paperback edition March 2018
www.sjmccoy.com

Cover Design by Dana Lamothe of Designs by Dana
Editor: Mitzi Pummer Carroll
Proofreaders: Aileen Blomberg and Marisa Nichols

ISBN 978-1-946220-35-6

Dedication

For Dana.

We talked about this one for so long and now he's finally here!

I want to thank you for being with me every step of this journey. You were the first person to read Emma and Jack's story – we've both come a long way since then.

You've captured every one of these books with your amazing graphics, giving every single one the right feel – I give these stories the words, you give them the pictures. They wouldn't be what they are without you.

Can you believe it's been five years since we started talking on Goodreads? So much has changed in that time. If you think about where we were then and where we are now – twenty-five books later – it's hard to believe.

I still have the first teaser you ever made, I remember telling you that YOU should do my covers – and you telling me I was nuts! Look at you now. ;0)

We've created twenty-five books, lived through a whole bunch of ups and downs, given birth to two successful businesses and we're only going from strength to strength. Out of everything we've created, the most important to me is our friendship, you've had my back, I've had yours and I know we will continue to do so, that this is a friendship that will last a lifetime.

So, without any more mushy bits, I hereby dedicate Oscar to you, my friend.

Love you

J

oxo

Chapter One

Grace scrambled out of bed at the sound of her alarm. She'd had to move that sucker way across the other side of the room. She groaned as she padded over to it and made it stop. Surely there was an alarm clock out there somewhere that had found the happy medium between a sweet little tune that lulled you back to sleep and a malicious buzz like hers that blared into your sleep-addled brain and set your teeth on edge. She really should look for one like that.

She made her way to the bathroom, cursing to herself at the conviction that her roommate, Louise was already in there. She tried the handle and relaxed a little when the door pushed open. That alarm needed to go. It set her nerves jangling before she even started the day. In the shower, she let water as hot as she could stand roll over her, then turned it down a little as she felt the tension recede. Maybe she needed to try yoga or something. She was turning into a stress ball, and she didn't like it. She needed to work on relaxation and thinking happy thoughts. Okay, maybe just positive thoughts, that'd be a good start.

Half an hour later she was out on the street, and she was on time. How about that? And it was Thursday already, the week was almost over—there was a positive she could appreciate.

"Morning, beautiful," Spider greeted her as she entered the coffee shop on the corner. "The usual?"

"Please, and I'll take one of those cinnamon scones as well."

Spider smiled as he rang up her total. "Let me guess, you woke up crabby, and you need some sugar to sweeten you up?"

She made a face. "I'd love to deny that and tell you that I'm just sweetness and light, but ..."

Spider laughed.

"Yeah, right. Never mind. You know me too well."

"I sure do, doll."

She blew out a big sigh. "I do my best."

"Nah, you're awesome just the way you are. Don't you let anyone tell you otherwise."

"Thanks." She took a gulp of her coffee and smiled. "I'll see you tonight."

"Okay. I'm expecting a good turnout, so the tips should be good."

"I'm banking on it. It's going to be close this month."

Spider shook his head. "You know you need to form a committee or something, get people to chip in, help with the workload as well as the cost. I bet we could get you on the local TV and ..."

Grace shook her head. "No. You know that's not my style. I can do it myself."

"I'm not saying you can't. I'm saying you shouldn't have to. People would love to know about the center; I'm sure there are plenty who'd love to help."

"Yeah, well, you help enough, and I appreciate it. I have to get moving. I can't be late for work. If I am, I'll be late back here."

"So, go! I'll see you later."

She had to run to catch the bus before it pulled away. Taking a seat, she sipped her coffee and forced herself to smile. What would be the positive take on that? She didn't miss the bus.

That was a good thing. She shouldn't be grumbling that she almost missed it; she should be thankful that she just caught it. She nodded to herself, her smile a little bigger—until the guy sitting across from her gave her a worried look. She wanted to laugh out loud as he changed seats, but that would only confirm his suspicion that she was a crazy. Instead, she pulled out her phone. There were already three emails from Harry. Two about accounts she was working on, and a third asking her to pick him up a coffee on the way in. She pursed her lips. She would, but she'd be taking the money for it straight out of petty cash—he'd forgotten to pay her back for too many little errands lately.

She got off the bus a stop early and finished her own coffee, tossing the cup into the trash can on the corner before picking up two more and walking the next block. When she reached the building which housed Harry Dressel, CPA's office she stopped outside the front door. A limo had just pulled up. That wasn't something you saw too often in this part of town.

"Do you think he's lost?"

She turned at the sound of the doorman, Sean's, deep voice, and even deeper chuckle. "Probably, but shouldn't you be inside sitting at the reception desk waiting, just in case he's coming in here? He could be the most important visitor you ever get. You don't want to screw it up."

Sean's eyes grew wide, and he stubbed out his cigarette before scurrying back inside.

Grace laughed to herself as she watched him take up his position at the front desk. He even dug out a hat she'd never seen him wear before and sat up straight. When she looked back at the limo, she sucked in a deep breath. Wow! The guy who'd just climbed out looked as though he was stepping straight out of the pages of a magazine. Damn. He was hot. A navy suit, white shirt, broad shoulders, narrow hips. And the way he walked. That must be what it was like to stride with confidence—she'd read that phrase in a book the other night and thought it was too cliché. Now she got it. She lifted her gaze back up, lingering on those narrow hips a little before taking in the broad chest again, and the shoulders, and ... Whoa. The face. How had she ever torn her eyes away from it the first time? Short dark hair, strong jawline, full lips, and big brown eyes. Eyes that were staring back at her. Eyes that ... oh, were getting closer, and were still locked with hers.

"Here, let me get the door for you."

Even the voice was sexy, rich, and deep and ... oops. He was now holding the door for her, and she was still standing there staring at him like a complete idiot.

"Oh. Thanks." Who turned the temperature up? She'd always wondered what it would be like to have a hot flash. Now she had some idea. As she stepped past him, the temperature soared. She could feel the goose bumps running down her arms and the shivers chasing each other down her spine.

Once she was safely inside, she hurried over to the elevator and stabbed at the button, hoping she could just step inside and be whisked away from her embarrassment. She didn't react like that to guys. She was more used to having that effect on them. She risked a peek over to Sean's desk. The guy wasn't there. She scanned the foyer in a panic. Was she going nuts? Had she just imagined him? No. He was still there, standing by the door—staring at her! What the ...? There was no way he'd felt it, too. She looked away as quickly as she could, but not before she saw the corners of his lips turn up in a knowing smile.

Grace started to tap her foot. Arrogant prick! He wasn't staring because she'd had the same effect on him. It was because he couldn't believe she hadn't noticed him. He probably had women fawning over him wherever he went—

looking like that, he had to. He was watching her to make sure she'd noticed him. He was gauging her reaction, to make sure she was swooning over him. Well, screw that! She jabbed at the button again, willing the elevator to hurry the hell up so she could get out of here before he joined her.

No such luck.

He strode to the desk. There really was no other word for it. He moved with the arrogance and grace of a big cat. No. Make that stealth, not grace. She didn't want her name associated with anything to do with a guy like that. Stealth sounded more sinister, and there was something sinister about him. She had to bite back a laugh. She needed to get a grip. He wasn't sinister looking at all. Watching him exchange a few words with Sean, he was friendly, warm. He got Sean smiling and nodding with him. She shook her head and turned back toward the elevator. Finally! It announced its arrival with a ding, and the doors slid open.

Once she was inside, she jabbed at the button again, this time trying to make the doors close. She really was shit out of luck this morning. Just as they began to slide together, a set of long, strong fingers slipped between them, and they slid open again. And there he was.

He stepped inside with a smile and a nod, then pressed to go to the eighteenth floor. Shit. That was her floor. He couldn't go there.

"What do you need?"

She stared at him blankly. "Need?" Could he somehow see inside her mind, see all the months of a dry spell that had gone on way too long? Or could he see the images floating inside her head? Images of what the two of them could do if the elevator somehow got stuck.

The corners of his lips curved upward again. That just might be the sexiest smile she'd ever seen. "Which floor?"

"Oh!" Well, wasn't she an idiot? Her mind raced. She couldn't get off the elevator with him. He might think she was following him. "Seventeen."

He hit the button, but before they started to move, the doors slid open again. Thank God for that!

Two men and two women came in and turned to face the doors, leaving Grace and the Big Cat alone in the silent space behind them. Grace gripped the tray with her two coffee cups and stared determinedly at the numbers above the door. She'd always suspected this was the world's slowest elevator, but this morning's ride confirmed it. Every second was torture. She could smell him—all citrus and man. She'd swear he was looking at her, but she refused to allow herself to sneak a peek. He'd catch her!

She tried looking down at the coffee cups, but that just made a strand of her hair fall across her face. She wrinkled her nose and tried to blow it away, then she froze. There were those long, strong fingers again. They brushed her cheek as they took the errant strand and tucked it behind her ear. If the heat had surged through her when he held the door open, then her blood was boiling in her veins right now. All the little hairs on the back of her neck stood up and sent shivers racing down her spine. Even her scalp tingled. She turned. How could she not?

Those big brown eyes were twinkling with amusement. "I hope I didn't overstep? You looked uncomfortable."

She shook her head mutely. What could she say, even if she could find the breath to speak?

The elevator stopped, and she silently begged the people in front of her not to get out. They couldn't leave her alone in here with this guy—she would not be responsible for her actions. To her relief, they didn't. Instead, two more got in, and that was quite a crowd. Everyone shuffled back a little.

She had no clue how it happened, but somehow, she ended up face to face with Big Cat. She was in the corner, and he was right there in front of her, staring down into her eyes, that quirky little smile playing on his face again. She'd had a laugh with Spider the other night when one of the customers had tried hitting on her in the coffee shop. She'd told Spider that her sexual desires were dormant. Hell, had she been wrong about that! Standing here, face to face with this guy, she discovered that her sexual desires weren't just active—oh, no, they were rampant. She was grateful for the tray of coffee she was gripping. It gave her hands something to do that kept them from reaching up to touch his face, maybe sinking into his hair or even sliding around his waist.

"Are you okay?"

She nodded rapidly, meeting his gaze briefly. Even she heard the gasp she made when he rested his hand on her hip. What was he doing? You didn't just do that to a stranger in a crowded elevator.

"Are you sure?" He looked worried now.

She looked down to where his hand rested on her hip. Except it wasn't his hand—it was the purse the woman in front of her had slung over her shoulder. Grace couldn't help it. She laughed. Wow, she needed to get laid. Okay, the guy was attractive, but he shouldn't affect her this badly. "I'm fine, thanks. Have a great day." She edged her way to the front and squeezed out through the doors before they had a chance to open fully on the seventeenth floor. She couldn't help it. She had to look back before they closed. He'd made his way to the front, too. He met her gaze with a smile.

Bye, Big Cat. She bid him a sad farewell. At least, in the real world, the world where she'd never see him again. She had a feeling her imagination would be seeing a lot more of him in the nights to come.

She smiled back at him; there was no harm now. And he winked! The arrogant prick actually winked at her. She stood there staring as the doors slid shut, and then he was gone. She chuckled and set out toward the stairs. She'd take them slowly to make sure he was gone by the time she got up there.

Her phone buzzed, and she set the coffee tray down on the little table that stood between the two sets of elevator doors. It was a text from Harry.

Forget the coffee. I don't need you till eleven.

Grace shook her head. Harry was a pain in the ass sometimes. If he didn't need her till eleven, why couldn't he have figured that out last night, for crying out loud? She could have slept in, taken her time—not wasted her money on a coffee he wasn't going to drink. She smiled, nope, she was going to stick with the positive thing. If this morning hadn't played out exactly the way it had, she'd never have laid eyes on Big Cat, and she'd hate to have missed out on their close encounter in the elevator. If she really wanted to look on the bright side, she could see that she now had two hours and two cups of coffee on her hands—and she intended to use them wisely.

Chapter Two

Oscar smiled to himself as he left Harry Dressel's office. That had gone well. He'd gone in expecting to meet at least some resistance, but the guy had rolled over easily. It was a win-win proposition for them both, and Harry knew it. He'd talked Oscar up from his initial lowball offer, but nowhere near as far as Oscar had been willing to go. Assuming they could get all the paperwork pushed through, in less than a month Oscar would own the lot and could start to build his second nightclub, and Harry Dressel would have a nice lump sum he could add to his retirement nest egg. Oscar looked around as he made his way back to the elevator. By the looks of this building, Harry's nest egg could probably use some help. He pressed the button and pursed his lips as he waited. Maybe something would turn up between now and the closing date that would force him to offer a higher price. He didn't want to rip the old guy off.

The elevator arrived, and he stepped inside, smiling at the thought of the girl he'd ridden up here with. She was ... what? Weird? Yep. Beautiful? Absolutely. Weirdly beautiful? Maybe that was it. She wasn't his usual type, but damn! He'd have loved to ride her in the elevator, rather than ride the elevator with her. He smiled to himself and hit the button for the seventeenth floor. He could take a quick look around. He might bump into her. He had no doubt that he'd be able to persuade her to come for a ride with him if he did. She'd caught his interest the second he'd stepped out of the car, and he'd half walked, half run to get to the door in time to open it for her. He wasn't one to trot after a woman; he didn't need to. He let them do the chasing and rewarded them handsomely when they managed to charm him into bed. She wasn't the kind who'd come to him, though. He'd instinctively known that, and so he'd gone to get the door for her. She'd breezed past him with no more than a thanks and a waft of coffee. Maybe that was why his cock had sprung to attention and hadn't completely settled back down even now. It seemed he and his cock were up for something different, and the girl with the coffee could be just the kind of challenge he was looking for.

He stepped out of the elevator on the seventeenth floor and looked around. It was a clone of the eighteenth floor he'd just left. A dingy hallway, a board with a list of company names and room numbers. He went to look at the board. What kind of work did a girl like that do? There was an advertising agency. Maybe she was the creative type? He'd love to find out—in bed, or in the back of his limo. He scanned the names. A law firm. No. Even one small enough to have offices here didn't hire women like her. He left the board and made his way down the hall, peering in windows as he went. There was no sign of her. He shook his head with a rueful smile. This was crazy. If he wanted to get laid, he could call any one of a dozen women who would happily oblige him at a moment's notice. Rich women, influential women, married women; all of them beautiful and all of them eager to do whatever he wanted. So, why in hell's name was he wandering around here looking for a chick who might not be open to anything he wanted—let alone everything—even if he could find her? He turned around and headed back to the elevator. This time he rode solo all the way back down to the lobby. He nodded at the doorman on his way out. For a second, Oscar contemplated asking him about the girl. No. He pushed his way back out into the sunlight on the sidewalk. He obviously needed to shake things up a bit, but he didn't need to go stalking office girls.

"How did it go?" asked TJ when he got back in the car.

"I couldn't find her." Shit! Why had he said that? TJ was asking about the meeting with Dressel.

TJ turned all the way around in his seat and peered through the little window at him. "Couldn't find who?"

"Never mind." Oscar grinned at him. "It really doesn't matter. What I meant to say is that Dressel happily accepted my offer, and I should be able to go ahead and buy the lot without any headaches. Six is about to gain a sister club."

"And what are you going to call it, Six Two, just like you?"

Oscar rolled his eyes. "No."

"How about Seven? This time you can get all the deadly sins in there?"

"No. Maybe Five and this time we'll leave out Envy as well as Sloth."

TJ laughed. "That sounds like a plan to me. From what I've heard Envy is the biggest cause of all the drama in there."

Oscar nodded. "It is. I need to do something about it."

"The only way you could do that would be to clone yourself. Then all the girls could have their own Oscar, and they wouldn't need to scratch each other's eyes out over you."

"Or maybe my brother could entertain at least a few of them for me, help me out?"

TJ's smile disappeared. His face hardened, and he turned back around. "Where to next?"

Oscar got out and walked around to the passenger seat. Once he'd fastened his seat belt, he punched TJ's shoulder playfully. "Sorry."

TJ shrugged. "You're not supposed to sit up front, you know."

"When have I ever followed the rules or done what I'm supposed to?"

TJ smiled grudgingly. "I guess. Let's just forget you said anything, and get back to pretending that I'm your driver, can we?"

Oscar nodded solemnly.

"So, where to next?"

"Back to the office."

~ ~ ~

Grace knocked on Harry's door at eleven o'clock on the dot. "Come in."

She pushed the door open with her foot and smiled at him over the tray of coffee and sandwiches she was carrying.

He narrowed his eyes at her suspiciously. "What's that for?"

She rolled her eyes. "The coffee's for drinking and the sandwiches are for eating."

He gave her a sour look. "You want to watch that smart mouth. It'll get you into trouble one day."

She sighed and put the tray down on the table. "And you want to watch that miserable streak of yours. It'll lose you your best employee one day." Usually, she could read Harry like a book, but she couldn't figure out what his problem was. The way he was looking at her was a mix of sadness, defensiveness, and irritation. "What's up, anyway? I'm trying to only think, say, do and be positive today. So, against my better judgment, I brought you an early lunch, and this is what I get in return."

He took off his glasses and set them down on the desk.

Uh-oh. That was never a good sign.

"Listen, Grace, take a seat."

She sat down and folded her arms across her chest, and her foot started to tap. This wasn't going to be good. She could tell.

"I have a feeling that today could well be the day I lose my best employee—and it won't be because of my miserable streak."

She frowned but didn't speak. If he was about to fire her, she wasn't going to make it easy for him.

"I agreed to a deal this morning that you're not going to like, but I want you to understand that it's a good deal for me."

What the hell was he talking about? And why wouldn't he just spit it out? "What deal?" she asked impatiently.

He sighed. "I had an offer on the lot on Gascoigne Street ... and I accepted it."

Grace's breath froze somewhere in her throat. He couldn't mean what she thought he did. "The lot? You mean, you're going to sell the land from under the center?" She shook her head, trying to clear the confusion. "I don't understand. Will we have to pay ground rent now, or ...?"

He shook his head sadly. "I'm sorry, Gracie. I am. But you know that lot was always meant to be my nest egg. I bought it at the very first mention that the neighborhood might take off.

Industrial chic wasn't even a thing back then, but with all the urban regeneration projects, I've known for a while that the sale of that piece of land would set me up for life." He gave her a grim smile. "And I was right."

She stared at him. "Who's buying it? What do I need to do? Did you discuss the center with them? Will we have to pay rent?"

He sucked in a deep breath and blew it slowly. "No. The center will have to go. He has plans to build."

Grace dropped her head and buried her face in her hands. She'd known it couldn't go on forever, but she hadn't expected it to end this soon. The center was nothing more than a run-down building, in a run-down part of town. Except, now, new businesses were moving in; new money was cleaning up old buildings, tearing some down, opening coffee shops and boutique clothing stores. She shook her head. A ramshackle community center didn't belong in the middle of that, but where would they go? The kids who came before school and after. The vets who gathered a couple of nights a week. The young moms who met in the afternoons. The older ladies who hung out to knit and do crafts together. She raised her head and met Harry's gaze. She couldn't be mad at him. It was the right move for him; she could admit that. And besides, there was no point wasting time being mad at him. It was more important to figure out what she was going to do.

"How long have we got?"

"He'd like to close the sale by the end of the month."

"Shit!"

"I can drag it out a bit, if you need."

She gave him a sad smile. "Thanks, Harry."

He shrugged. "You don't have to pay me anything for this month."

"Thanks." Harry had never charged any rent for the use of the building. They had to pay for maintenance and insurance, but he only covered his costs.

"What are you going to do?"

She shrugged. "I have no freaking idea. I think I need to let it sink in, then I'll figure something out."

"Take the rest of the day off."

She looked at him in surprise. "You don't need me?"

"You need the time to get to grips with the news, and with what you're going to do, and ..." He picked up his glasses and turned them over and over.

"And what?" Why did she have the feeling the other shoe was about to drop?

"And after the sale closes, then no, I'm not going to need you. It'll give me enough to finally retire."

All the air rushed out of her lungs. Wow! A minute ago, she'd thought her biggest problem was losing the center. Now she realized she was going to be losing her job, too. Awesome! She got to her feet.

"I'm sorry, Grace," said Harry as she reached the door.

She turned around and nodded. "It'll be okay. Don't be sorry; this is what you've been working your whole life toward."

He gave her a weak smile. "Thanks. I don't like to screw you over in the process, though."

She shrugged. "Any time someone wins, someone else has to lose. Tell me something?"

"What?"

"Who's buying it and what do they want it for?"

"It's Oscar Davenport."

Grace stared at him, none the wiser.

"You've never heard of him?"

"Should I have?"

"I guess not. He's big money. He built and sold a couple of tech companies. Last year he opened a new nightclub downtown, Six. It's a big success. He wants to build another one."

Grace let out a bitter little laugh. "So, some bigshot asshole who already has more money than he needs, is going to build a nightclub where he and his friends can play, while all those people who use the center as a lifeline are going to be shit out of luck?"

Harry looked uncomfortable, but Grace was too angry to care.

"I'll see you tomorrow." She managed not to slam the door too loudly as she left. So much for being positive. She'd tried today, she really had, but look how the day was turning out, and it wasn't even lunchtime yet. She took the elevator back down to the lobby and shook her head at the memory of Big Cat. He might have had her squirming in her panties, but he was probably one of the people who hung out at that stupid nightclub. Who called a club Six anyway? What kind of name was that? And what did it matter? When the elevator doors opened, she stalked out through the lobby. She needed to get back to the coffee shop. Spider would listen—she didn't expect that he'd know what to do, but he'd listen, and he'd help her brainstorm.

"What are you doing here?" he asked when she walked in and pulled up a seat at the counter.

She rested her elbows on the counter and her chin in her hands. "You're not going to believe me."

"You lost your job?"

"Not yet, but I'm only going to have it for another month."

"Shit. What happened? I can't believe Harry fired you. He wouldn't be able to run the place without you."

She shrugged. "Exactly. He doesn't plan to run the place at all anymore. He's going to retire."

"Damn. I thought that was just a dream. I mean he's always talked about retiring, but I never thought he'd be able to afford to."

"Well, he had an ace up his sleeve the whole time, and he just played it."

Spider poured her a coffee and slid it toward her. "What ace?"

"The land."

"The land where the center is?"

"Yup. He just sold it."

"Holy shit!"

"Yeah, that's what I thought, too. Apparently, some rich guy is going to tear it down and build a nightclub."

"Damn." Spider came around the counter and took a seat beside her. "It's like a piece of our history—a piece of us—is going to be demolished."

"Yeah. I'm not so worried about the past. It's dead and gone, and we survived. I'm more concerned about the present—and the future of all those kids who use it now."

Spider nodded. "And the vets."

"Yup. I don't know what I'm going to do."

Spider scowled at her. "What do you mean you? What are we going to do? Why do you always have to be so independent? You're not the only one who cares about that place, you know. You're not the only one who has a stake in what happens."

"Sorry." She made a face. She wasn't really sorry. It was easier for her to operate on the assumption that she was the only person she could count on—and Spider not only knew it, but he of all people understood why. They were both products of the foster care system. They'd both survived some pretty horrific situations. The adults who were supposed to have been there for them had failed them at every turn. They'd both aged out of the system and, like half the other kids in their situation, had found themselves homeless within six months. The center had been a lifeline for both of them—in different ways at different points in their lives. It had been a place to go after school. A place to eat when they were on the streets. It'd never had all the proper licenses and registrations, so officially it wasn't a shelter, but they'd both spent colder nights sleeping there. Just like some kids and vets still did now.

"Do you think there's any way we could stop it from happening?"

"No." She sighed. "I considered it on the bus ride back here. There's probably some way we could put the guy off, convince him that it isn't the right place for a nightclub, but there's no point. If he doesn't buy it, someone else will. And I couldn't do it to Harry anyway. To him, this is like winning the lottery. Except he can take a bit more credit for the outcome. He spotted a long-term investment, and he went for it."

Spider nodded. "Yeah. He's been as generous as he could afford to be. Anyone else would have charged rent all these years."

"Yup. We have to face the fact that we need to find a new place."

"How? Where? Come on Gracie, be real. The whole point of the place is that it's in the neighborhood—and there's no way we could afford anything in the neighborhood anymore."

"Well, if the neighborhood's changing that much, where's everyone going? The center needs to be where the people who need it can get to it."

Spider shrugged. "I dunno."

"Neither do I, but it seems to me that everyone's still hanging in, in the apartments around there. The kids are still at the same school we went to."

"But there's no way we could raise the money to rent anything around there."

"So, we get creative. Maybe everyone takes it in turns to have everyone over?"

"Come on, most of them don't have a place and the ones who do couldn't fit more than a couple people inside."

"I know. I'm just trying to get some ideas rolling. What have you got?"

"I dunno, doll. I ain't got shit."

She patted his shoulder. "We'll figure something out. And you can't say you ain't got shit—"

"Would you give up trying to fix the way I talk?"

Grace laughed. "Slow down. I wasn't trying to correct you. I meant you do got shit! Look at this place."

"It's no palace."

She grinned at him. "Don't be so modest. It's your own business. Your own place. You done good, Spider Webster. You've risen up against the odds, and you've built something. I'm proud of you."

Spider was a big guy, muscular, good-looking in a tattoos-and-beard, rough-around-the-edges kind of way. Most people would never believe he had a big soft heart, but Grace knew he did. She could see it shining in his eyes as he made aww-shucks noises and pushed her arm before getting down from his seat and going back behind the counter.

"You're the one who should be proud of yourself, doll. I've done okay for myself, but you've done so much good for so many people."

Her smile faded. She knew he was saying he was proud of her, too, but if the center was about to disappear, there wouldn't be anything left to be proud of. She'd feel like she'd let everyone down. And Spider was only half right; he had done more than okay for himself. But her? She'd been too focused on keeping the center going to worry about herself. She had nothing to show for the years of hard work she'd put in. The few things she owned were in the room she rented from Louise because it was cheap, and in another month, she wouldn't even be able to afford that since she'd be out of a job.

Chapter Three

"So, what's the plan for this new club of yours?" asked TJ.

Oscar poured them each a glass of bourbon and came back around the bar to join him on the sofas in the VIP area. They'd fallen into the habit of having a drink here in the club at the end of the workday and before the worknight began. Oscar took a slug of his drink and shrugged. "More of the same. More drinking, more debauchery, more good times to be had. Another place to see and be seen for the rich and the beautiful. A place where those who've earned it can gather and enjoy it."

TJ made a face.

"And there goes the disapproval again."

"I didn't say a word," protested TJ.

"I can hear your thoughts. I can smell the disdain in the air. Not everyone has your high ideals, you know. Some people just want to kick back and have fun."

"I know. I don't expect anyone to live by my standards. I know better than that. But I just don't get it. It doesn't suit you. I mean, I know you love to play, you're all about the good times and having fun, but you only play so hard because you work so damned hard. From what I've seen so far, the people who come in here aren't the ones who work hard, they're the hangers on and the wannabes. They're more about looking rich than being rich."

"You judge too harshly. They just want to have fun."

TJ held his gaze. "Tell me this, then. When was the last time you had a conversation in this club that engaged you, that caught your imagination, let alone your intellect?"

Oscar shrugged. "Not for a while. Probably only with you or with Hope and Chance when they were here." He smiled. "And Clay McAdam when he played here."

TJ laughed. "Don't you see? We're all people who you know anyway. Your brother, your cousin, and some country superstar dude who you know because … go on remind me, how the hell did you and the granddaddy of country music get to be friends?"

"We did a big charity auction together a few years ago, and we got to talking. He is one smart man. He might come off all down-home, down-to-earth country boy, and I guess he is, but he's no country bumpkin. He's one of the very few minds I respect—in business and in life."

"I get that, and he's also not the kind of guy who would come into a club like this just for fun, is he?"

Oscar shrugged. He was getting irritated with this line of questioning. He knew exactly what his brother was getting at. The nightclub business wasn't really him. It had been a new challenge and one that he'd risen to and conquered. Six was a big success, but it was hardly fulfilling his life's ambition—not that he knew what that was. "So, what do you think I should be doing?"

"I have no idea. You're the genius in the family. You figure it out. I'm just surprised that you're planning to build another one. I don't get it. You did what you set out to do. You opened a club; you made it the hottest spot in LA. You proved once again that there's nothing you can't turn your hand to and turn into a success. Why aren't you moving on to something new?"

"Because I think a whole chain of nightclubs would be good."

"Fair enough. If it's what you want to do, then more power to you. I just thought you'd move on to something else."

Oscar nodded and took another drink of his bourbon. He'd thought he'd want to move on to something else, too. Six had been a whole lot of fun to set up and to brand. It hadn't taken long to grow a following and a name in the LA nightlife scene. He'd thought it'd be a stopgap, a breather after he stepped down from running the hedge fund—that had been way too stodgy for him. He'd made huge profits for a bunch of fat cats and they'd still wanted him to proceed with caution—and worse, they talked about him like he was their boy genius. He'd hated it.

He'd thought by the time Six was truly successful, he'd have found his next project, but he hadn't, so he was simply going to repeat the process. Something would come to him soon. He'd wake up at three in the morning with some crazy hare-brained scheme that no one would believe he could pull off, and he'd spend the next year or so proving that he could. He just wished that moment of inspiration would come soon. "I'll move on to something else when I know what it is. Until then, I'm in the nightclub business. What about you? Are you anywhere near ready for your next step, whatever that may be?"

TJ pressed his lips together and shook his head. "No."

"Okay." Oscar knew better than to push it. "I just wanted to make sure that you're still happy enough playing chauffeur for me."

"It suits me just fine." TJ drained the last of his bourbon then met his gaze. "I appreciate it."

Oscar smiled. He wished he could do more for his brother, but TJ could only move at his own pace. After all he'd been through, on his last deployment and since he came back, it was major progress that he was getting out of bed every morning and showing up for work—and staying sober so he could drive Oscar around. "Do you have any plans for the weekend?"

"No."

"Do you want to make some?"

"Like what?"

"Well, Hope and Chance are going to be in town. They're coming in here on Saturday night. Maybe we could all have lunch or something?"

TJ pursed his lips.

"I think you'll like Chance, and you know Hope would love to see you."

"Let me think about it?"

"Of course." It was more than Oscar had expected.

"Tell me something?"

"Anything." Was TJ finally going to open up?

"When you came out from seeing Dressel today, and I asked you how it went ..."

Oscar chuckled. "And I told you I couldn't find her. You want to know what the fuck I was talking about, right?"

TJ rewarded him with one of his rare smiles. "Damned straight I do. What she? And why would you have found her in there?"

"Okay, just because it's so good to see you finally smiling, I'll admit what a prick I am. When I went in there, there was this chick going in ahead of me. She was ..." He smiled as he remembered her: her long, dark hair, the black top she'd been wearing and the purple tights. He shook his head.

"She was what?"

"Weird, gorgeous. Curvy."

TJ gave him a puzzled look. "You saw a woman that interested you in there?"

Oscar nodded slowly. "Yup. And you're right. She wasn't my usual type. She was ... I don't know...there was this tension between us in the elevator. She was all raw energy and ..." He shrugged. "When I got done with Dressel, I went to see if I could find her, but I couldn't."

TJ laughed. "You had a missed connection with an office girl?"

Oscar laughed with him. "I guess I did. What does that tell you?"

"It tells me that even your dick knows you need a change from the kind of women who hang out in clubs looking to get laid and get their claws into rich guys."

"You never miss the chance to ram your point home, do you?"

"No, but I wasn't even trying. It's just so obvious. If you were happy with the life you've set up, you wouldn't have noticed a girl like that, not when you've got LA's most beautiful parading though here every night."

Oscar sighed. "I guess, but come on. It's not like life is terrible or I'm failing or anything. I'm just coasting for a while till I find my next challenge."

"Yeah, just hurry up about it, can you?"

~ ~ ~

Grace set the last tray down on the counter and blew out a
sigh. Spider had been right when he'd predicted a good
turnout, and it had been one hell of a busy night. If she wanted
to salvage the last shreds of her positive thinking, she could
admit that he'd been right about the tips, too.

Spider smiled at her. "Take a load off and have a beer."

She wasn't about to argue. She climbed up on one of the
stools and took a long drink of the cold beer he handed her.
"Thanks."

"Hey. You've earned it."

She nodded. She had. What had started out a while back as
Spider and his buddies jamming a couple nights a week had led
to the coffee shop becoming a popular venue for local bands.
The place had been packed out all night, and she'd been
rushed off her feet.

The crowd had left now. She and Spider were cleaning up.
Amber and Josie were, in theory, still helping, but they were
focusing on the area around the little stage at the back where
the band was still packing up. Spider shot them a dark look,
but Grace waved a hand at him. "Don't give them a hard time.
We're pretty much done, anyway."

"I suppose."

They both looked up as the front door opened. It was Grace's
roommate, Louise. She looked amazing. Grace sneaked a
sideways glance at Spider and wanted to tell him to reel his
tongue in. There was no point, though; he always looked like
that whenever Louise showed up.

"Hey, girl."

"Hey." Louise came and pulled up a seat beside her. "Sorry I
didn't make it till now."

"No worries. Do you want a beer?"

"Thanks, I'd love one."

"Let me guess," said Grace as Spider turned away. "You had a date, but he bored you?"

Louise laughed. "I did, and he did."

"You should have just come in here. You wouldn't have been bored," said Spider.

Louise smiled as she took the beer. "You can't say that. You wouldn't have had a minute for me."

It amused Grace to see her big, burly buddy look bashful, but at the same time, it irritated her a little that Louise toyed with him the way she did. Louise was one of those people you couldn't stay mad at, though. She was pretty and sweet, she didn't have a mean bone in her body. She was just a bit clueless about the effect she had on guys. Grace pursed her lips; either she was clueless, or she pulled off the dumb blonde act very convincingly. No there was no guile to her. Grace was just being cynical.

"And what's up with you?" Louise asked. "You don't look too happy."

"She got some bad news today," Spider answered for her.

"Oh, no. What?"

Grace shrugged. She'd been trying not to think about the center tonight, hoping that maybe her subconscious would mull it over and surprise her with a flash of brilliance. "Harry's selling up and retiring. The center's going to be torn down, and I'm going to be out of a job. So, you might want to start looking for a new roommate."

"Oh, that's awful. I'm so sorry. There must be something you can do to save the center? And don't you worry. I can carry the rent for a while. I know you'll find another job in no time."

"Thanks, Lou." Grace regretted her less-than-charitable thoughts of a few moments ago. Louise really was as sweet and kind as she seemed. It was Grace who was the cynic.

"But what happened? Who's bought it? And why is it going to be torn down?"

"Apparently, it's some guy who owns nightclubs. He's going to build a new one there. I suppose it makes sense. The whole neighborhood is on the rise."

Louise nodded sadly. "I hate to say it, but it is. A new nightclub would fit right in with everything that's going on. Do you know the guy's name?"

"Oscar Davenport."

"Ooh!" Louise's eyes lit up momentarily before she stopped herself. "Sorry. I know this is terrible for you, but have you seen him? He's dreamy."

Spider groaned and turned away to finish cleaning up.

"Sorry." Louise looked suitably contrite. "If you saw him, you'd know what I mean. I bet there's a photo of him in one of my magazines. I'll show you when we get home. But what's more important is that the guy is like a billionaire. And he does all kinds of work with charities. I'll bet you could talk him into helping you relocate the center or something."

Spider had rejoined them and was looking hopeful. "That's a great idea, Louise. Rich people make all kinds of donations to charity—they can write it off. Maybe if we can show him how much people need the center, he'll want to help."

Grace's mind was racing. "More like, we might be able to persuade him if he thinks he'd get a lot of bad press by tearing the center down."

"But how?"

Louise might not understand, but Spider nodded his understanding.

"The media would be all over a story like that," said Grace. "Thanks, Lou. You just came up with the best idea so far."

Louise looked baffled. "But what ...? How ...?"

Grace smiled grimly. "Don't you worry your pretty head."

Spider raised an eyebrow. "What are you going to do?"

She shrugged. "Hopefully nothing, but I'll bet we could whip up a media frenzy if we wanted. And if he thinks that, too, he might be more open to helping us out somehow."

"So, are you going to see him?" asked Spider.

"I was thinking I could get a number and call him."

"No. We should go and see him. Everyone knows he's always at Six on Saturday night," said Louise.

Grace cocked her head to one side, not understanding.

"Six is his club downtown." Louise looked her over. "You'll have to wear something of mine, but we'll get in."

Spider laughed at the look on Grace's face. "Do it. It's a bold move, but you're nothing if not bold. Venture into the lair of the enemy—take the fight to him."

"Okay." Grace blew out a sigh, wondering what she was getting herself into. It was the only plan of action that had been put forth so far, though, and she wasn't one to sit around and do nothing.

Chapter Four

Oscar leaned on the end of the bar and surveyed the club. It was a typical Saturday night. The drinks were flowing, and the dance floor was starting to fill up. People were having a great time. He sighed. He knew TJ was right. This wasn't him. Well, it was him; he loved to party, and he loved to have fun. But he needed to have more going on in his life. He needed to be building a business, pushing boundaries, overcoming challenges. He wasn't getting any of that here. He smirked when he spotted Kendra Parson weaving her way through the crowd toward him. He could get some of that, but she wouldn't present any kind of challenge.

"Oscar," she purred when she reached him. "Is it my lucky night? Have I managed to find you all alone?"

"Kendra." He leaned in and allowed her to peck his cheek. Her hand rested briefly on his shoulder, telegraphing her intent through his body as a little shiver, which surprised him when it managed to elicit some interest from his cock. He straightened up with a smile. Maybe it was her lucky night. "I have some company." His words had the effect he'd expected. She pouted a little and the site of her bottom lip sliding out confirmed that, yep, his cock was interested in some playtime.

He shook his head at her. "Now, don't look like that. I have family in town. I have to visit with them for a while. But maybe later …"

Her smile returned on full beam. "Oh. In that case." She flipped her long blonde hair over her shoulder. "You can look for me later. I might still be here."

Oscar nodded. He didn't call her out on it, he was too much of a gentleman, but they both knew that, if he didn't go to find her, she'd be here when the doormen threw out the last of the stragglers.

He glanced over her shoulder. He wasn't lying, he really did have family visiting, and they'd just arrived. He raised a hand to wave at them before excusing himself.

Kendra reached up to kiss his cheek again. He was a little disappointed that the spark of interest seemed to have fizzled out, but maybe it'd return later.

"Hopey!" he exclaimed as he reached her and her husband, Chance. She wrapped him in a hug, and he held her close for a moment. His cousin was one of the few people whose mind he respected and whose company he enjoyed. When she let him go, he reached out to shake with her husband, Chance. As they shook, Oscar grinned and pulled him in for a man-hug. He hadn't known what to make of Chance at first, but they'd clicked and were building a kind of unique friendship that Oscar truly valued.

"You know we can't stay for long," said Hope.

"I know you could stay as long as you want, but you don't want." He winked at Chance. "I know it's not your scene, but I wanted us all to have dinner together."

Chance smiled through pursed lips. "I can endure it, for you."
He turned and scanned the dance floor. "But we get to eat in
the quiet room upstairs, right?"

"Chance!" Hope slapped his arm, but Oscar just laughed. "We
do. Come on. The table's ready."

"Is TJ coming?" asked Hope.

"No. He said he'd come to lunch tomorrow if you want to
meet up, but this isn't his idea of fun."

Chance smirked at him but spoke to Hope. "I think TJ's going
to be my favorite of your cousins."

Oscar laughed, but then a thought occurred to him and he met
Chance's gaze. "You might be right about that. I think the two
of you might get along. I think you'll be able to connect with
him on a level I can't."

Chance's smirk disappeared, and his eyes narrowed. "Hope's
told me a little about what he's been through. I don't know
that I can be of any use to him and there's no point me
sticking my nose in. I'll talk to him if he wants to talk to me."

"Yeah, that's all I meant."

Hope gave him a warning look, and he changed the subject as
they made their way upstairs to the quieter restaurant area.
"How's the baby doing?" He led them into one of the private
dining rooms while Hope chatted away about the little one.
Once they were all seated, he realized that Chance was
watching him intently.

"What's up?"

"Nothing. I'm just trying to figure out what you're going to
say."

"About what?"

"We want you to be his godfather!" Hope beamed at him.

"You do?" Oscar wasn't too sure what that entailed, but he didn't think it was anything like the Pacino version.

"We do."

"If you want to," added Chance.

"I'd love to. It'd be an honor." He nodded at the waiter. "I think this calls for champagne."

~ ~ ~

Grace surveyed herself in the mirror. Louise had performed some kind of miracle. She peered at her face; it didn't even look like her. She rarely wore makeup, and now she was covered in the stuff, but it didn't feel bad—and it looked fabulous, she wasn't going to lie about that.

Louise beamed at her. "What do you think?"

"I love it, Lou. Thank you."

"You're welcome, and what about the dress, are you comfortable? You look fantastic. You should keep it. It doesn't look right on me, but it's as if it was tailor-made for you."

Grace couldn't stop smiling. The dress was gorgeous. It was the stereotypical little black dress, but damn. It fit her in all the right ways in all the right places. Even if there wasn't enough room in it for her to take deep breaths. She turned around to check out her rear view, and Louise laughed.

"Is it wrong of me to say I love your booty? I never knew you had such a great ass!"

Grace laughed with her. "Neither did I. I always thought it was this round thing that followed me around and needed to be hidden under long shirts, but damn, that thing is big and beautiful!"

"It is. You know people spend hours in the gym trying to make their ass look like that; some people even get implants and butt lifts and everything. And you? You just hide in your tunics and then when you need it, you unveil the best booty in all of LA."

"Ha. I wouldn't go that far."

"I would. Anyway…" Louise checked her watch. "We should get going."

Grace checked the clock on the wall. "It's only eight-thirty. I thought we weren't going until nine."

Louise didn't meet her gaze.

"Oh no. You've got a date, haven't you?"

Louise gave her a half shrug. "Not exactly a date, no."

"Then what?" Grace knew she looked the part but getting dressed up like this and going to some fancy club wasn't exactly in her wheelhouse. She'd been glad that Louise was so eager to go with her. She didn't need her, or anything, but …

"I said I'd meet Graham in there. I thought you'd get busy talking to Mr. Davenport and I'd be at a loose end."

Grace blew out a sigh. "More like you'll get busy with Graham, I won't be able to get near Davenport, and I'll be at a loose end."

"No. I won't abandon you. Whenever you're ready to leave, you come find me, and we'll share a cab home."

"What, you, me and Graham?"

"Maybe," Louise gave her a coy smile.

"Thanks, but I'll do what I've got to do and get out of there. You just get me in."

"We'll have no problems there, not with you looking like that."

"And you looking like that." Louise was so pretty, she was wearing a deep blue dress that was simple and elegant and sexy as hell. She gave a little twirl. "Thank you, but I'll be in your shadow tonight."

Grace laughed. "As if that'd ever happen."

"I'm serious."

"Whatever. Can I just practice walking in these shoes a bit more? I don't want to fall off them and make a fool of myself."

"Okay but hurry up about it. I'm going to call a cab."

When the cab pulled up outside Six, Grace stepped out and straightened her dress. She turned to wait for Louise and almost fell, forgetting that she was wearing the stupid heels.

Louise caught her arm. "Careful."

"I told you I needed more practice."

"You'll be fine. Here. Link arms with me and we'll just sashay straight up to the doormen."

Grace took in the long line of people waiting. "You mean, walk right by all of them and expect Muscles at the front there to just lift the rope for us? No, thanks. I'd sooner go to the end and wait in line."

Louise sighed and took her arm, steering her toward the front. "Have a little faith in me, would you? I know I'm not much in the practical world, but you're in my world now."

Grace reluctantly teetered along beside her. If she'd been in her own shoes, she might have pulled away, but in these heels, she didn't dare. She relaxed a little as Muscles, the doorman on the left, caught sight of them and smiled.

"See," said Louise. "It's Brandon. He goes to my gym."

"Of course he does," said Grace with a chuckle. She should have known. Her seemingly air-headed roommate had friends all over the city—people she'd met at the gym, on the bus, in the grocery store, anywhere and everywhere.

"Lou-lou!" Brandon, formerly known as Muscles, grinned as they reached him. "How's my favorite girl?"

"Wonderful, thanks. How about you? It's so nice to see you." She put her hands on his shoulders and stood on tiptoe to kiss his cheek. Grace was shocked to notice that he was checking her out over Louise's shoulder. She dropped her gaze and fumbled in her purse.

Louise turned to her. "Grace, this is my friend, Brandon. Brandon, I'd like you to meet my roommate, Grace."

Grace lifted her gaze and held her hand out to shake with him. He grinned at her and before she knew what he was doing, he'd wrapped her in a bear hug. "I gotta say the pleasure is all mine, Grace."

She might have to disagree with that as she caught her breath and stepped back, teetering on her heels again. Wow. "Nice to meet you, too."

Brandon lifted the rope and let them pass. She was aware of the indignant grumbles coming from those at the head of the line. She wanted to apologize; she knew how it felt to be where they were. She wasn't used to being on this side.

Brandon rested an arm around her shoulders as he walked them through the foyer. Louise raised an eyebrow at her and grinned. Brandon was a big, good-looking guy, and normally Grace wasn't shy around men like that, but tonight he was a distraction. She was here on important business. As Brandon slid his hand down her arm before leaving them, she did a double take, she'd swear she'd just seen Big Cat from the elevator, weaving his way through the crowd. She needed to get a grip. He'd featured in her fantasies the last couple of nights, but she couldn't start imagining him when some other guy touched her. That wasn't healthy—not healthy at all. She turned to look back at Brandon and smiled. If she wanted to ditch the fantasy man and come back to the real world, Brandon wouldn't be a bad place to start. He grinned at her and nodded. She knew where to find him when she was done here.

"Oh my God, Gracie. Brandon took a real shine to you. Should I give him your number?"

"No, but you can give me his."

"Oh, of course. I love the way you do that; you're so empowered."

Grace laughed. "Empowered?"

"Yes. You never give a guy your number, but you take his. Then you're the one in control, and you don't ever sit around by the phone wondering if he'll call. You call your own shots."

"It's just sensible if you ask me." She looked around. The place was crowded. "So, what's the plan?"

"I said I'd meet Graham out on the terrace at nine-fifteen." Louise checked her watch. "We've got time to get a drink first."

"I didn't mean that. I mean what we came here to do. I can't believe that we got so carried away with all the hair and makeup and dresses, that I forgot one crucial detail."

"Oh, no. What?"

"I didn't make you show me a photo of him. I can't leave you to your night with Graham until you help me find this Oscar Davenport."

"Oh, shoot! How about you get us a drink, and I'll wander around, see if I can spot him."

"Okay. Meet me back here in five minutes."

Grace returned to the pillar to meet up with Louise after getting their Cosmos—two very expensive Cosmos. She took a teeny sip of hers. It was heavenly, but she was going to have to make it last all night. Louise came hurrying back to her.

"Did you spot him?" She handed Louise her drink.

"Yes, but I think he was leaving!"

"What?" That hadn't been part of the plan. The guy was supposed to be here in his club. It was Saturday night. "You think he was, or you saw him leave?"

"He might have just been walking some people out. He was with a couple. I think it was Hope Davenport and her husband. Have you seen him? The cowboy from Montana?"

Grace shook her head impatiently. She didn't give a rat's ass about some cowboy. She needed to catch up with Oscar Davenport before he left. "Which way?"

Louise pointed toward the foyer.

"Hello, beautiful."

Grace groaned. Just at the worst moment, Graham had shown up. Louise wasn't going to be any use now. "What does he look like?"

"What? Oh. Sorry. Gorgeous! He's good-looking. Dark-hair, broad shoulders, he's got a light beard, and he's wearing a navy suit."

"Thanks." Grace set out across the foyer. There was no point trying to get anything more from Louise. She was already in happy, smiley, chatty mode with Graham. She stopped when she neared the doors. There were plenty of people milling around, but none who fit Oscar Davenport's description. Awesome. She'd give it five minutes, and if she didn't find him, she'd down her Cosmo and leave. She took another sip. Or maybe she'd stick around a while and have another. They were so good.

She leaned against a pillar and observed the comings and goings. She felt bad as she saw the couple who'd been at the front of the line come in. She hated that some people got a free pass in life while others had to stand and wait. She was used to having to stand and wait, but she still hated the inequality when she was on the other side for once.

So, this was how the other half lived, huh? She watched them talking and laughing and smiling. Mostly it was people coming in, some standing around, presumably waiting for others to join them. They all looked so wealthy. It wasn't just that they were dressed up; it was more than that. They had that air about them. And good luck to them. She might hate random inequality, but she didn't begrudge anyone what they made of their lives. Live and let live.

She looked over at the entrance where there were three sets of double doors. Had Oscar Davenport already left through one of them, or was he about to walk back in? She looked down a hallway that ran off to the left away from the main entrance. There were three people standing there talking. The woman was beautiful; she had long, honey-blonde hair and the figure of an athlete. Grace pushed away from the pillar and stood up straight. There was her first clue. Louise had said she thought she'd seen Hope Davenport. She used to be an athleticwear model—Grace knew that much. And, given that she shared the last name, she must be related to Oscar. The guy standing beside her, his arm slung around her shoulders, didn't look like he fit in totally. He was dressed the part—and he was hot— but he had a rugged look about him. Maybe he was the cowboy husband. The guy they were talking to had his back to her, but he had dark hair and was wearing a navy suit. She set out toward them. She had to take her chance.

She watched as he hugged the woman and shook hands with the guy, and then they left. She hurried as best she could to the entrance to the hallway, so the guy would have to pass her when he came back in.

He turned around, and she stopped dead, almost falling off the stupid shoes. Big Cat? It couldn't be the guy from the elevator? It was! She leaned against the wall to catch herself, and he looked up. All the air rushed out of her lungs as he met her gaze. He recognized her, she could see it in his eyes. And she knew it for certain when the arrogant prick winked at her.

He strode toward her, closing the distance between them far too quickly for her to catch her breath. Big Cat was Oscar Davenport? The guy she'd been fantasizing about was the same guy she'd been hating?

He stopped when he reached her and stood way too close, looking down into her eyes, even though the shoes made her three inches taller than usual. "We meet again."

Damn. Even his voice was sexy—just as deep and rich as she remembered. "We do." She considered telling him she was just leaving. She could go home, get her head around this turn of events and find him again when she wasn't so thrown off balance—by the shock or the shoes.

He was looking deep into her eyes; his smile was wicked—there was no other word for it. She stared back, unable to drag her gaze away. No guy had ever affected her like this. Her breath was coming low and shallow; her nipples had stood to attention; she could feel them—she just hoped he couldn't see them. He reached out his hand, and she automatically responded, offering hers to shake with him. The moment those long, strong fingers wrapped around hers, all the electricity that had hummed in the air between them in the elevator zapped through her body. Every nerve ending tingled. His eyes widened. Did he feel it, too?

"Have a drink with me?"

She nodded. What else could she do? He took hold of her hand and led her through the crowded main room. Part of her wanted to pull away; part of her was grateful for something to hang onto. Most of her was just reeling with shock and something else ... desire? Was that what it was?

As they made their way up the stairs, she tried to shake herself out of this trance he'd put her in. She was here to talk to the guy who was going to take the center away—not to get it on with the guy from the elevator.

Chapter Five

Oscar's heart was pounding as he led her up the stairs. He couldn't believe his luck. The girl from the elevator was here in his club—and she was even hotter than he remembered. He took a deep breath as they reached the top. He was fully aware that there might be more than luck at play here. People in this city knew who he was. His face had been in enough magazines and celebrity TV segments. She might well have recognized him and come here to find him. He smiled as he turned to her. All the better for him, if she had. The kind of girls who did that—and she wouldn't be the first—all came looking for one thing, and in her case, he'd gladly give it to her.

She seemed to waver on her feet, and he put his hand on the small of her back to steady her. "Are you all right?"

She nodded. "I'm fine." She sounded almost angry. He raised an eyebrow and was rewarded with a beautiful, genuine smile. "If you must know, I'm having trouble staying upright in these shoes."

He glanced down at her feet. They were sexy-as-sin heels—the kind he liked to think of as fuck-me-pumps. He'd be happy to oblige. But the messages she was sending were all wrong. The kind of girl who came to him looking to get laid would never admit they couldn't stand up in high heels.

"Upright is overrated, if you ask me. I prefer horizontal." He had to test her out. Was she going to giggle and swoon, and give him the answer that his cock desperately wanted?

Hell, no.

She scowled at him. "I'll let you get back to that, then. You were the one who asked if I wanted to have a drink with you."

He grinned. Spirited, huh? He liked that. "And I'd like you to. Please?" He jerked his head toward one of the private rooms and gestured with his hand for her to go ahead of him.

She hesitated for a moment; he could see the struggle in her eyes. He was relieved and a little surprised when she went ahead of him. He'd half expected her to turn around and leave. He raised a hand to one of the waiters and mouthed bourbon to him before following her into the room and closing the door behind him.

She spun around at the sound of the door closing and wobbled as she did. He stepped toward her and caught her arm, crowding her a little more than he needed to. He wanted to tell himself that he was just testing for her reaction again, but it was more than that. His body acted of its own volition, wanting to get as close to her as he could. His cock was straining in his pants, but that was less surprising than the way his arms closed around her, wanting to hold her to him.

She stepped back a little too fast, but luckily for her, the sofa was right behind her, and she plopped down on it with a surprised little uff sound.

He stood over her, some primal part of him sorely aware that her lips were at the perfect height for her to ... He turned around at the sound of a buzzer.

She jumped back to her feet and stared around wildly. "What was that?"

"The doorbell." He went to open it and let in the waiter who set a tray down on the table beside the sofa. A bottle of bourbon, two glasses, and an ice bucket. "Thanks," Oscar nodded at him, and he left.

The girl looked up at him. "How did you know I drink bourbon?"

"I didn't. Lucky guess, I suppose."

She eyed him warily. "Did you know I was coming?"

That intrigued him. "Why would I? And you know that leads to the question of why you're here."

She nodded reluctantly. "Do you want to pour me one of those before we get down to that?"

Oscar poured himself a glass and then looked up at her.

"Neat."

He hid his smile as he fixed her drink. His first impression had been right; she wasn't his usual type. There was no airy, flirty chatting with this one. She was blunt and to the point. What he wanted to know was what her point was. Why was she here? And why did she suspect that he already knew about it?

He took a seat on the sofa and patted the space beside him.

She pursed her lips, considering it. He could see the moment she reached her decision, and she sat down and took the glass from him. She knocked it back and set the glass down on the table.

He watched her for a few moments. When he waited long enough, people talked just to fill the silence. She didn't.

"So. Did you come here to find me?"

She nodded.

He couldn't stop the corners of his lips from quirking upward.

"Don't look like that. I didn't know you were you."

He gave her a puzzled look. He had no idea what the fuck that meant.

She shrugged but didn't elaborate.

"Well, I'm glad you came."

"You are? Why?"

"I felt like we had a missed connection the other day. I couldn't get you out of my head."

"Seriously?"

"Yes." Maybe he could get her to open up more if he did the talking to start with, got her to relax. He rested his hand on her knee. His intent had been to get her to soften toward him, but it only made him harder. He wanted to slide his hand up her thigh, under her dress, and between her legs. Dammit. He smiled and focused his attention on her face. "Seriously."

She shook her head. "You're just full of shit, aren't you?"

He threw his head back and laughed out loud. "Yeah. I guess I am, in general, but I'm not shitting you about that. I've kept thinking about you, hoping I could find you again. I even went down to the seventeenth floor to look for you on my way out."

"Why? You've got a club which is full of beautiful, and no doubt willing, women every night of the week. What's so special about me?"

"You're beautiful, you're different, there's a strength about you, an I-don't-give-a-shit air to you that I find irresistible."

She shook her head and poured herself another bourbon—proving him right, the women he brought in here usually waited for him to refill their glass.

"You found me irresistible, too, didn't you? That's why you're here."

She let out a short bitter laugh and shook her head. "If I'd known you were you I probably wouldn't have come."

What the hell was she talking about? She wasn't making any sense. "So, why did you come?"

She met his gaze. "I'm not sure I want to tell you."

He wasn't sure if she was a crazy, or if she was playing him somehow, but he couldn't resist going along with her. "How about I persuade you to tell me?"

"What do you mean?"

He took her glass from her hand and set it down on the table then leaned closer. Her full red lips had been tempting him since he'd first seen her at the end of the hallway. "I can be very persuasive," he breathed as his hand slid farther up her thigh and leaned in closer still. He lowered his lips to hers and then stopped less than an inch away. "If you want me to."

She nodded and closed the final distance between them.

~ ~ ~

Alarm bells were ringing in Grace's head, but they couldn't pierce the fog that had descended on her brain. He'd leaned in ninety-five percent of the way. Some magnetic force drew her the last five. He brushed his lips over hers, and his hand moved up her thigh. Some tiny part of her mind tried to direct her hand to push him away; instead, it diverted course and reached up to cup his head, pulling him down closer for more. He obliged, tangling his fingers in her hair and tipping her head back. She moaned as he dropped his lips to her neck and nibbled the soft spot behind her ear. All the muscles in her stomach and lower tightened, making her seek out his lips with hers. With his fingers caressing her thigh and him nibbling her neck, she was terrified he could make her come right there and then. She had to divert him back to a kiss. It worked. He cupped her face between his hands and crushed her lips with his. He slid his tongue inside, and she was a goner. She could feel herself moan as he claimed her mouth. The alarm bells managed to pierce through with a dead certain realization that he could claim her whole self just as easily if she let him.

She broke away abruptly. This wasn't what she'd come here for. She edged away from him, aware that she was breathing hard, and there was no hiding just how aroused she was. She slowly lifted her gaze. Would he be angry? Guys who were used to getting what they wanted didn't like it when a woman called the shots—she knew that. Would he be mad? Or would he dismiss her since she wasn't proving to be the easy lay he'd obviously thought she was?

The last thing she'd expected was to see a look of amusement on his face. Was he laughing at her?

"You don't like it?"

She pursed her lips. She wasn't a liar.

His smile grew wider. "Good." He handed her the drink, and she downed it. She needed it after that.

"Are you going to tell me why you're here?"

"Well, I didn't come here planning to spread my legs for you, if that's what you're thinking."

He chuckled. "The thought had occurred; you wouldn't be the first."

Arrogant prick. She scowled at him.

"I'm sorry. I'm an asshole when it comes to women." He poured them both another and ran his hand through his hair—a gesture that for some reason had her squirming in her wet panties. In that moment all his arrogance was gone, and he was even more attractive.

"Why?" She couldn't resist asking.

He met her gaze and shook his head. "No one ever asks why. Usually, they either agree or tell me that I'm not, that I'm just misunderstood."

She let out a short, harsh laugh. "They play you, just the same way you play them, then. I'm not interested in playing the game. I'll just say it like I see it. You're an arrogant prick, and yep, you can be a real asshole when it comes to women."

His expression changed. "You're not here to get vengeance for a girlfriend I've fucked and forgotten, are you?"

She pursed her lips. "No. I'm speaking purely from personal experience and projecting a general assumption from there."

"Fair enough. I'd say it's a logical assumption." He winked at her again. He really needed to stop doing that. She wanted to hate him for it, but there was something so damned sexy about it.

"Do you get lots of vengeance visits?" she asked, just to move past the wink.

He shrugged. "There have been a few. I don't understand why women can be so vindictive. I'm always up front; I like sex, and it's all I have to offer. I'm not going to call you afterward, and if you come back in here, you will see me with someone else."

She stared at him. There was no way on earth she'd tell him, but she thought that was admirable, at least the fact that he'd admit it. Most guys pretended to be interested in more just so they could get a girl into bed. Honesty was a much better policy, as far as she was concerned.

"So, are you interested?"

"What?" Her head jerked up, and she met his gaze. She'd thought he was explaining why some girls got mad at him, not laying out his terms for her.

He chuckled. "I had to ask."

"And I have to say no."

He heaved a big sigh and looked up at her with big puppy dog eyes. "Aww, are you sure?"

She tried to hide a smile, but she couldn't, not completely. He was gorgeous, and he played it so well. If the future of the center wasn't on the line, there was no way she'd have been able to resist him. She shook her head. "I'm sure."

"In that case, are you going to tell me why you're here?"

She stared at him for a long moment, then finally shook her head. This was all wrong. She'd come here with two options that she could see. If he seemed like a nice guy, she'd planned to appeal to his better nature, and see if he'd be interested in making some kind of donation to help rehouse the center. If he seemed like an asshole, she'd thought it'd be easy to make some veiled threats about going to the media with the story of how he was ousting kids and vets and single moms. She'd figured that would be enough to make him throw some hush money their way or maybe even get him involved—looking for good press instead of bad. Now she didn't know what to do. He did kind of seem like a good guy, but at the same time, he was, by his own admission, an asshole. And besides, none of her contingencies had accounted for him being Big Cat, the arrogant prick from the elevator, and they certainly hadn't factored in the possibility of her kissing him, or him asking if she wanted to have sex—or her desperately wanting to. "No, you know what? I'm just going to leave. I will need to talk to you at some point, but this is neither the time nor the place." She got to her feet.

He scrambled to join her. "You haven't even told me your name."

"Grace."

He chuckled. "Amazing Grace."

She sighed. "I thought you might be more original."

He shrugged; his cocky smile was back. "You've thrown me off. I admit it. You win this round."

She smiled. It was good that he thought so. She was feeling like a failure, but she needed to figure out a plan of attack before she put anything to him; if she tried talking to him now, she'd get nowhere—except maybe underneath him.

"Can I call you?"

She shook her head. She wasn't playing hard to get. She was just making sure she stayed in control. Growing up the way she had, she'd felt powerless about so many aspects of her own life. These days, she did whatever she could to stay in control—empowered, as Louise had put it.

He gave her a puzzled smile. "You're serious, aren't you?"

"Absolutely."

He grinned. "If I give you my number will you call me?"

She took his card with a smile. "When I'm ready."

Chapter Six

By Thursday morning, Oscar was growing impatient. He hadn't expected Grace to call him on Sunday, that was too soon. Monday had been a possibility, but he hadn't been too surprised not to hear from her. Yesterday, he'd smiled every time his phone had rung—and had been disappointed every time it wasn't her. He'd gone to bed in a bad mood and had stared at the ceiling for twenty minutes. He'd almost called Kendra—she could have helped relieve some of his frustration, but she wasn't what he wanted.

TJ popped his head around the office door. "Are you busy?"

"No. Come on in. What's up?"

TJ came in but didn't take a seat. He never seemed able to relax long enough to sit down. "I was going to ask you the same thing. You've been Oscar the Grouch this week. Is something wrong?"

Oscar smiled. TJ hadn't called him that since they were kids. "No. Nothing serious anyway. I'll tell you if you want a laugh."

His brother raised an eyebrow. "I'm intrigued."

"Remember when we went over to see Dressel to make the offer on Gascoigne Street?"

"Yeah."

"Remember when I said I couldn't find her?"

"The office girl?"

Oscar gave him a rueful grin. "Yeah."

"What about her?"

"She was in here on Saturday night."

TJ groaned. "And you slept with her, and now she's stalking you?"

"No. She refused to sleep with me."

TJ gave him a skeptical look.

"She turned me down." Oscar shrugged. He didn't want to admit, even to himself, just how big a part that played in his frustration.

"I know you're not used to hearing no from the ladies, but seriously? That's enough to put you in a bad mood?"

"No. It's not just that. She came in here looking for me. But she didn't expect me to be me."

"What the hell does that mean?"

"I'm not sure I know. From what she said, I think she came here looking for Oscar Davenport."

"Well, yeah, that'd be you."

"No, listen." He needed to spell it out, not just for TJ's sake, but so he could get a better handle on what she'd meant. "She said she probably wouldn't have come if she'd known I was me."

"I ask again—what does that mean?"

"I think it means, that she was looking for me as Oscar Davenport, but she didn't know that the guy she'd met in the elevator was Oscar Davenport. I think it was some kind of weird coincidence."

TJ's eyebrows knit together. "Let me see if I've got this straight. On Thursday, the two of you had some kind of missed connection in an elevator. Then on Saturday night, office girl goes out looking for Oscar Davenport, and gets the shock of her life when she realizes that Oscar Davenport just happens to be the same guy she already met a few days earlier."

"Yup."

"And why was she looking for you?"

"I don't know. She wouldn't tell me."

TJ shook his head. "That makes no sense."

"I know, but it kind of does. She was looking for me to tell me something or ask me something, then she discovered I was the guy from the elevator, and that threw her off." He smiled as he remembered the way her lips had parted to let him kiss her, the way her fingers had sunk into his hair.

"Are you sure you didn't screw her? The look on your face says you did, and that might explain why she left without telling you what she came for."

"No. I did try to persuade her." He grinned at TJ. "And it almost worked, but she came to her senses and walked out on me."

"So, why haven't you tracked her down and figured it out? If it's bothering you, do something about it."

Oscar brought his hand up to his face and rubbed his thumb across his lips to cover the smile that was playing on them. "This is the part where you get to laugh at me."

"Because?"

"Because she said she'd call me, and she hasn't yet."

TJ laughed. "Man, that's got to be a first."

"Yeah, I think you're right. It is. And I don't like it; it's frustrating as fuck."

"It'll do you good."

"You think?"

"Yeah, I do. She'll call you before the week's out."

"I hope so."

TJ laughed. "I do, too. It's good to see you put in your place a little, but I prefer the happy, cocky version of you to the sour, grumpy version."

"Okay. Point taken. I'll put her out of my mind. Do you want to grab some lunch with me, help distract me?"

"Sure. Let's go."

~ ~ ~

Grace stood in Harry's doorway. "Do you need anything else before I leave?"

"No, thanks. You go on."

"Okay, I'll see you tomorrow."

Harry held her gaze. "I've been asking around for you, Gracie. I'm confident I can help you find something before I close the doors here."

"I know. Thanks, Harry. I'll find something. Don't you worry about me. You need to focus on making plans for you and Susan. I bet she can't wait for you to retire."

Harry made a face. "She's not as thrilled as I thought she'd be. She seems to think I'm going to be under her feet."

Grace chuckled. "It'll take some adjusting to, I'm sure, but you'll love it. Both of you. Anyway, I need to get going. I need to get over to the center."

Harry pressed his lips together and sucked in a deep breath. "How's it going?"

She shrugged. "We're doing what we can to raise money. The church over on Driscoll has a room we can rent a couple of times a week, but it's not cheap, and it won't work long term."

Harry looked uncomfortable.

"I'm only telling you because you asked. Don't look like that. We'll figure it out. It's not your responsibility. You've done more for the place than most people ever would. Don't feel bad because you can't keep it up."

"Thanks, Grace."

She nodded. "See you tomorrow."

She got off the bus right outside the center, just as she had most days for what felt like most of her life. She still couldn't wrap her head around the fact that in a few more weeks it'd all be over. Time was running out, and that thought made her finger the card in her pocket. The card she'd carried with her ever since he gave it to her on Saturday night. She needed to call him. She couldn't afford to waste time just because she didn't want to seem too keen to talk to him again. This was about so much more than that.

She pushed on the front door and almost fell through it as someone on the other side opened it at the very same moment.

Spider caught her.

"Are you falling for him?" asked Reese who was coming out with Spider.

She shook her head. "Nah, I've got better taste than that, and he wouldn't have me even if I did."

Spider nodded. "You're right there." He made a face and shuddered. "It'd be like doing my little sister."

Grace laughed. "Yeah, err no."

Reese eyed them both. "Sometimes I wonder. You two seem like you'd make a great couple."

Grace and Spider both laughed. People often said that, but she didn't see him that way. Spider was the closest thing to family she'd ever had. Her dad had died when she was a few months old, and her mom had gone on to have more boyfriends and more kids. Grace didn't even know how many half brothers and sisters she had. There'd been four of them when child services had come for them, but she'd heard there were more after that. She looked up at Spider. "No. We have way too much history for that." It was true. They'd first met when they were both in the same foster home. It'd been a rough one, to say the least. Spider had looked out for her, and to his surprise at first, she'd looked out for him. They'd been sent to different homes after that but had gone to the same school. "Are you guys leaving already?"

"Not yet. We're just unloading. Do you want to help?"

She followed them back out to Spider's van. He'd started expanding the kitchen at the coffee shop a couple of months ago, and now he delivered sandwiches to the center whenever he could.

"What have you got going on tonight?" he asked as he handed her a tray.

"Dinner by the looks of it," she said, as she eyed a sandwich.

He scowled at her. "You know I'll feed you anytime you come in."

"And you do, but I'm not just going to come strolling in for food when I'm not even working."

He shook his head. "I don't see why not."

The three of them carried the trays back into the center. Grace smiled and nodded as she went. People broke away from their conversations and got up from their seats to follow them through to the kitchen area. This would be the first time that most of them had eaten today. Grace stood back and watched with a smile as one of the kids grabbed the donut she'd had her eye on. It'd do him more good than it would her.

Spider caught her eye and shook his head with a smile.

"Hi, Grace." She turned to greet Terry, one of the vets who'd started coming in last winter.

"Hey, Terry. Did you get a license for that thing yet?"

He made a face and turned the wheels of his wheelchair, zooming toward her and then spinning away at the last minute. He whirled back around and gave her an almost toothless grin. "Nope, it's more of an off-road vehicle, but I've got the hang of it."

She laughed. "You sure have."

Terry was a Vietnam vet. From what she could gather, he'd been living on the streets for more than a decade. When she first met him, she'd thought he might have severe mental health issues, but it turned out that he just chose to act crazy to keep people away. He didn't like people, didn't trust them, in general. Grace could relate to that. He'd walked with a stick but could barely get around. The first morning she saw him, she'd arrived at the center just as he was sneaking out. She'd tried to talk to him, but he'd gone full-blown crazy acting. When he finally limped away after yelling and screaming at her, she'd followed him a little way, offered him her coffee and when he took it, said, "I guess I'll see you tomorrow then." He'd met her gaze and nodded, and their friendship had grown from there. It had been solidified for life when Grace had found the wheelchair advertised for fifty bucks on Craigslist and bought it for him. Of course, she'd told him it had been donated to the center, but that was just to avoid both their embarrassment, and he knew it.

"Have you spoken to Davenport yet?" Terry's steely blue eyes were piercing.

She wanted to look away, but she wouldn't. "No. I'm going to try him tomorrow."

"And what are you going to say?" asked Spider, who she hadn't realized had come over to join them.

She sighed. "Don't give me a hard time—either of you."

"Wasn't about to," said Terry. "I'm just waiting and watching. I've never seen you get uptight like this about anything. I want to see how it plays out."

Spider met her gaze. "I do, too, but we're running out of time."

"I know, I know. I wanted to give it a day or two—"

"Yeah, but it's already been four."

She sighed. "I just wanted to be sure. I wanted to do some more research on the guy. From what I've learned, he's totally aboveboard. I think any kind of threat would be the wrong move. We need to appeal to his better nature and ask him for help."

Spider gave her an evil grin. "And you hate that because you want the guy to be an arrogant prick, right?"

She scowled. "No! Why would I hate it? I want what's best for the center, and if he's a good guy, then hopefully he'll help out."

"So, why don't you go ahead and call him?" asked Terry.

Spider smirked at her.

"What's your problem?" she asked.

"I don't have one. Your problem is that you think I'm stupid. I know what's going on."

Grace held his gaze, hoping that her scowl would make him back down, but it didn't work.

Spider grinned at Terry. "See, this Oscar Davenport guy is a bit of a ladies' man. From what I've heard, he's not just a billionaire, but a hot, sexy billionaire who knows how to show a girl a good time. Right, Grace?"

"I wouldn't know. And what would it matter? My only interest in him is whether or not he's going to do anything to help the center."

"Not true," said Spider.

"Yeah, I'm not buying it." Terry smiled at her. "It's the pink in your cheeks that gives you away."

Grace huffed. "What the guy looks like has nothing to do with anything."

"Maybe, maybe not." Spider turned around to watch a couple of the kids who were arguing over one of the sandwiches. "I think it does, but either way, call him soon, would you?"

Grace nodded, and he left them to go and break up a fight before it started.

"Are you worried he'll be more interested in you than in helping?" asked Terry.

Grace laughed. "No. A guy like that—who can have any woman he wants—isn't going to be interested in me. Honestly, I'm just a bit embarrassed that I found him so attractive. I want to make sure I've got a lid on that before I approach him about the center. I don't want to screw up."

Terry sighed. "You're not going to screw up. You never do, at least not when it comes to the center. Just don't screw yourself over if you like the guy."

Grace raised an eyebrow at him. "What, you're into giving out romantic advice now, Terry? I didn't think that was your bag."

The way he smiled made her wonder. "You think you know me, Gracie, and you do better than most, but you don't know all of my story."

"Maybe one day?"

"Maybe, but don't turn it around on me. Call the guy tonight, and when you do, think about yourself as well as the center." He held her gaze for a long moment, his steely blue eyes searching her own. Eventually, she nodded.

"Good girl." He spun his wheelchair around and left.

It was almost nine by the time she got home. "Hello?" she called as she closed the door behind her. She didn't think Louise was here but wanted to be sure. She'd made the mistake before of coming home and getting comfy, curled up with a movie, only to see Louise and some guy emerge from her room.

There was no reply, and no giveaway noises coming from Louise's room. Grace blew out a sigh of relief. If she really was alone, then she had no excuses left for putting off making the call to Oscar Davenport.

She went to the fridge and got herself a cold beer. Taking it over to the sofa, she pulled his card out of her pocket. She'd decided she was going to keep this as brief and businesslike as possible. He might not even remember who she was. She was going to call him, tell him about the center, and how his building a new nightclub was going to affect it, and then ask if he'd be interested in making a donation to help them find someplace else. That was it. Nothing else. A shiver ran down her spine at the memory of his kiss—the way his hand had slid up her thigh. The way his tongue had explored her mouth. She closed her eyes for a moment, reliving it. Damn. She had to stop that.

She took a long drink of her beer and tapped his number into her phone. Keep it brief. Keep it businesslike. Spell out what she wanted and tell him she'd call him on Monday to see what he thought. That was all she had to do. So, why were her hands shaking?

She stared at her phone for a few moments. No. She wasn't going to waste time. Fantasizing about him wasn't an indulgence she could afford. She hit the dial button and waited.

Chapter Seven

"So, what do you think?" asked Oscar.

Julia Lawson smiled. It was an uptight smile. He'd bet she'd take some loosening up, but she'd be worth it.

"I think it's a great opportunity, Mr. Davenport. I'd love to work with you."

"It's Oscar, remember?" He rested his hand on the small of her back and guided her back toward the bar. The club was starting to fill up, but for some reason, he didn't want to use that as an excuse to take her into his private room. Instead, he pulled out a seat for her at the end of the bar and then stood in close. She was starting to relax a little, and when she flipped her long, blonde hair over her shoulder and smiled up at him, he knew she was starting to play the game.

He probably shouldn't be playing it. She was one of the architects he was considering for the new club. She was good—one of the best—and he admired her work. He also admired her ass—he closed his eyes briefly—it was a great little ass, even if it paled in comparison to the full, round ass that had been haunting him since Saturday night. Grace. Grace whatever-her-name-was had the best ass he'd ever seen. He wanted some of that ass. He wanted Grace.

"… Don't you think?"

He looked down at the architect. She was smiling at him, encouraging him; it was subtle, but she was. She wasn't to know that subtle wasn't his thing, and she sure as hell wouldn't dream that she couldn't hold his attention because he was too busy fantasizing about an office girl and her big, gorgeous ass. He gave the architect—Julia, that was it—an apologetic smile. "I think you have some great ideas. Give my office a call when you've put something together. I'm sorry, I have to talk to someone." He pulled his phone out of his pocket and showed it to her as if it could explain. He didn't need to make a call. He just needed to get away from her, to get somewhere quiet where he could let his imagination run wild. Grace had been plaguing his thoughts for days now. He'd kept pushing her away, but if she wasn't going to leave him in peace so he could indulge in Julia, then he was going to at least have to let his imagination have its way with her.

As Julia looked down at his phone, it rang. He gave her an apologetic shrug as he walked away. He didn't recognize the number, and his heart started to pound. It was Grace. He knew it.

"I was just thinking about you," he answered, as he strode over to one of the private dining rooms and let himself inside.

The line was silent for a long moment, but he waited. She wouldn't hang up on him; he knew it.

"What were you thinking?"

Damn, just the sound of her voice had him hard and aching for her. He leaned back against the door and decided to tell the truth, see where it took them. "I was thinking about your ass and what I'd like to do with you."

"Excuse me?"

"No, I wasn't thinking about excusing you."

Her voice was low and husky when she finally spoke again. "What were you thinking about?"

He smiled. "Come over here, and I'll tell you."

"No." She answered too quickly. She was open to the possibility, he could tell.

"You want to talk to me, don't you?"

"No. Yes. I mean, of course, I do. I wouldn't have called you if I didn't."

"So, come here. I can't hear you very well on the phone. It's a bad line. The club's noisy."

"It's nine o'clock."

"So?"

"So, by the time I get changed and get a cab over there, it'll be ten o'clock, and I have to work tomorrow."

"Then, don't get changed. I'll come to you. Where are you?"

"I'm not giving you my address."

Oscar smirked. "Okay, where will you meet me?"

She was silent for a few moments. "Can't we just talk on the phone?"

"What? Sorry? The line's really bad. Where did you say I should meet you?"

She sighed. "The coffee shop, on the corner of Wilson and Oak. Meet me outside in fifteen minutes."

"I'll be there."

Oscar chuckled to himself as he hung up. He couldn't believe his luck. It was like he'd wanted her so much he'd somehow magicked her up. He let himself back out of the dining room and headed for the office. He was glad TJ wasn't driving for him tonight. Darren would take him wherever he wanted to go and wouldn't ask any questions.

He looked up as Oscar entered the office. "Is everything okay?"

"Better than okay. Get the keys. We're going out."

~ ~ ~

Grace hung up and stared at her phone. That hadn't gone like it was supposed to. It wasn't her fault. He'd thrown her off, answering the way he did. He was just thinking about her? He'd taken her breath away when he said that, and she still hadn't recovered.

She jumped to her feet. Why had she agreed to meet him? And why the hell had she only given herself fifteen minutes? What kind of lunatic was she? She ran into her room. What was she going to wear? She'd said she didn't have time to change, and he wasn't expecting her to so she couldn't put on anything nice—even if she had time. She opened her closet and stared desperately at the few things she had. Jeans—jeans were always good. She pulled out her favorite pair, she knew she looked good in them—uh-oh she also knew her ass looked great in them. Had he really been thinking about her ass? She pulled out a long cream-colored sweater. It was roomy, and long enough to cover her ass, but still pretty. She ran into the bathroom and checked her face. Eyeliner, lipstick, check. That was as much makeup as she ever usually wore. If he expected her to look like she had on Saturday night, he'd be disappointed.

She grabbed her purse and headed out. It was only a five-minute walk to the coffee shop. She still had another five minutes to spare when she got there. She went inside and relaxed a little when Spider looked up at her with a smile.

"Are you going to let me feed you? I noticed you didn't get anything earlier."

"No, thanks. I'm meeting someone."

His eyebrows knit together. "Anyone I know?"

"Yeah, but it's not what you think." When she dated a new guy, she usually brought him in here at the beginning or end of the first date. Spider was the only family she had, and he liked to play the big brother role. Grace secretly loved feeling that she had someone in her corner, someone looking out for her.

"Who?"

"Oscar Davenport."

Spider chuckled. "I knew it."

"You don't know a thing. I tried calling him, but he was at the club, and he couldn't hear me, so he suggested we meet up to talk instead."

"Yeah, right. So, you're meeting him in here. Am I allowed to join in?"

"Umm, no. I'm meeting him outside."

Spider smirked. "And where are you going?"

She shrugged.

"I'll make you a deal, doll. You bring him in here before you leave, and I'll let you get on with it. You don't, and I might have to make things clear to him."

Grace stared at him. "It's not a date."

Spider shrugged and rolled up his sleeves, revealing muscular forearms that she knew the ladies loved, but she also knew sent a very different message to men.

"Okay, okay. I'll bring him in. For two minutes."

Spider jerked his chin toward the front window. "You'd better go get him then."

Grace followed his gaze.

"I don't know anyone else who'd show up here in a limo."

Grace's heart pounded in her chest as she walked to the door. She needed to get a grip. No matter what he might think of her ass, this was about the center. Nothing else. She stepped outside at the same moment he stepped out of the limo. He was just as gorgeous as she remembered— more so, maybe. Tonight, he was wearing dark jeans and a black shirt. She had to consciously stop herself from licking her lips.

He held the car door open for her, but she shook her head.

His cocky smile faltered but only for a second. "You don't want to come?" The glint of amusement in his eyes told her that yes, the double meaning was intended.

She nodded slowly. She wasn't going to admit to that yes out loud. "I need you to meet someone first."

"Who?"

"A friend. He's like a big brother. He keeps an eye out for me."

She was surprised when he smiled. "It'd be a pleasure."

As he came toward her, the driver's door opened, and a huge guy climbed out. "Everything okay, boss?"

"It's all good, Darren. We'll be with you in a minute." Oscar opened the door to the coffee shop and let Grace go ahead of him.

When they reached the counter, Spider adopted his best intimidating stance. Grace wanted to poke him in the ribs to make him deflate his puffed-out chest a little. "Spider, this is Oscar Davenport. Oscar, meet Spider." She pursed her lips. "Also known as Mr. Paul Webster."

Oscar reached across to shake Spider's hand. "Nice to meet you."

Grace hid a smile as she saw him grimace. Spider was no doubt giving him the famous bone-crushing shake.

"Nice to meet you. I won't keep you. Just wanted to see your face and to let you know Grace has people here, looking out for her." He didn't smile; there was nothing friendly in his face as he spoke.

If Grace didn't know him so well, she'd be terrified. She looked at Oscar. He wasn't worried. He held Spider's gaze and nodded, then he handed over his card. "I understand." He extended his hand again, and Grace knew what he was doing. He wasn't a glutton for punishment; he was making a point.

The hint of a smile on Spider's face as they shook again told her he appreciated it.

"Okay." She released the breath she hadn't known she'd been holding. "Are you ready?" she asked Oscar.

He nodded and gestured for her to go ahead of him. She wasn't sure if he was just that much of a gentleman or if he wanted to watch her ass.

"Ring me when you get home, Gracie," called Spider as they reached the door.

She shot him a grin. "Will do."

Oscar held the car door open for her, and she slid in. She looked around as he went to the other side to let himself in. She'd seen plenty of limos around, but she'd never been inside one before. It was fancy. The leather seats were soft, and the trim was all genuine wood.

Oscar slid into the seat beside her with a smile.

"Where to?" asked the big guy sitting up front.

"Home."

Grace's throat went dry. Home? They were going to his place? She turned to look at Oscar.

"We need to ... talk, right?"

The way he paused before he said talk, sent shivers down her spine. She nodded. They did need to talk. That was all this was about. She had to ignore or forget or somehow disregard the effect he was having on her. It didn't matter that the butterflies had taken to flight in her stomach. It didn't matter that the electricity in the air between them was practically humming. All that mattered was that they should talk about the center and that she should somehow persuade him to help them out.

He pressed a button on the armrest and the little window to the front slid shut. Grace pressed her lips together and closed her eyes. The center. She just had to keep focusing on the center.

"Don't you want to know any more?"

She gave him a puzzled look. It was hard to look at him and not smile. He was so handsome. His big dark brown eyes sparkled with amusement. His lips quirked up in the hint of a smile. "Know what?"

He brought his hand up to his mouth as if to cover his smile. She watched, mesmerized as he ran his thumb over his lips. For a crazy moment, she wanted him to run it over hers. "When I told you I was thinking about you, you asked me what I was thinking."

Oh. Shit. Yeah. He'd said he was thinking about her ass and what he wanted to do. She swallowed. Hard. "Maybe you should wait your turn. I had something I wanted to tell you on Saturday, and we haven't gotten to that yet."

He smiled. "Not my fault. I asked you to tell me."

She nodded. "True, but I don't like to be rushed." She accompanied the words with a meaningful nod, hoping he'd get the hint to go a bit slower.

He smiled, seeming to take her words as a sign that she might be open to whatever it was he was thinking if he took his time about it. "Okay. Tell me all about it. Why did you come looking for Oscar Davenport?"

She took a deep breath. She had to tell him. This was what it was all about. Just as she was about to speak, he reached across and tucked a stray strand of hair behind her ear. The electricity in the air zapped through her, doing strange things to her stomach, and lower. She turned to meet his gaze, and he smiled. "I couldn't resist. You do something to me, Grace."

She bit the inside of her lip. Why wouldn't he make this easy? In any other circumstances, she'd be thrilled that such a rich, good-looking guy wanted her. But this wasn't right. He wanted something from her—and wasn't making any attempt to hide it. She wanted something from him, and she had to tell him about it before anything else happened. The last thing she wanted was for this to end up seeming like a trade-off. She'd done a lot of things she wasn't proud of in her life, but she wasn't about to start using sex to get what she wanted—and she sure as hell didn't want him thinking that was her plan.

She straightened up and leaned away from him. "Don't."

He withdrew his hand, and his smile disappeared. For a second, she thought he was angry to be rejected, but his eyes were full of concern. "Forgive me. I thought …"

She shook her head. "You thought right. Come on. I'll bet you've never met a woman who wasn't attracted to you. I am. I'm not going to lie, but that's not what this is about. It's more important than that."

He cocked his head to one side. "What is? Tell me."

"Okay. You put an offer on a lot on Gascoigne Street last week."

He frowned. "How do you know that?"

"Because I work for Harry Dressel, and I run the community center that currently occupies the lot you're buying."

It was Oscar's turn to sit back. "I see."

"No, I don't think you do see. When we met in the elevator last week, you must have been going to see Harry to make the offer."

"But you work on the seventeenth floor."

She rolled her eyes. "I work on the eighteenth—for Harry. But you were already going to the eighteenth floor, and I didn't want to say the same floor as you."

He smirked. "Why not?"

"I don't know. I was stupid. I didn't want you to think I was following you or something."

There went the cocky grin again. "That's not stupid. It happens."

"I'm sure it does. But the point is, when I got to work after he'd met with you, I found out that he's selling the lot that he lets us use. The center is a lifeline for so many people in the neighborhood. I don't know what they're going to do without it."

Oscar frowned. "So, what, you're going to ask me not to buy it?"

She shook her head impatiently. "That was my first thought, but I know it's not realistic. It's Harry's way to retire, and besides, if you don't buy it, someone else will. I just ... well, I've done my research on you. You seem like a good guy. I kind of want to throw myself on your mercy and ask if there's anything you can do to help."

"Like what?"

"Make a donation, to help us find a new place, or at least to rent space."

He looked deep into her eyes, making her feel he could read the truth of her soul through them. "Why would I want to do that?"

"Maybe you won't, but I had to try. I had to see if you care about a bunch of latchkey kids, single moms, retired folk, and vets. I have to do something, so they'll still have a place to go. I figure people like you donate to charities for a tax write-off. I thought maybe you could donate it to the people you're throwing out."

He nodded slowly.

Had she blown it? She had no clue. His face wasn't giving anything away. She waited, but it was driving her nuts.

The car pulled off the road into a driveway where a big electronic gate swung open. She hadn't been paying attention to where they were going, but they were now in a very high-end neighborhood. The limo crunched up a gravel driveway and came to a stop in front of a beautiful, Mediterranean-style mansion.

She turned to Oscar, who still hadn't spoken. "Do you want me to leave?"

"Leave? Hell no!" His cocky grin was back. "Why would you leave? We're just getting started."

Chapter Eight

Oscar poured them each a drink and handed Grace one. She took it with a curt nod, making him smile. She wasn't like any other woman he'd ever brought here. There hadn't been many of them; he preferred to keep his playmates away from his personal life. The ones he'd brought back here were women he'd bonded with in some way or another—some way that went beyond the physical. He wasn't sure what kind of bond he and Grace had, but there was something about her. Did he want to fuck her? Absolutely. But there was something more than that.

She looked up at him from her seat on the sofa. There was something more than just the sexual going on between them but, right now, he was acutely aware of the fact that her lips were at the same height as his zipper again. Her long, dark hair hung loose around her shoulders, and it would be so easy to tangle his fingers in it as she took him in her mouth. No. He took a drink of the bourbon and got a grip. She'd come to him for help. That was the first thing they needed to deal with. He bit back a smile at the thought that maybe she'd want to reward him if he did. If he could please her, maybe she'd please him.

He sat down beside her and blew out a sigh. "Can I start by apologizing?"

She looked wary as if she thought he was setting her up somehow.

He reached out and took hold of her hand. "I'm not a bad guy, Grace. I may be a little misunderstood." He shrugged. "Or not. I like to play, and I play hard." He couldn't resist letting his gaze travel over her body as he said that. "But that's only because I work hard. I put all of myself into everything I do."

She met his gaze and raised an eyebrow.

He chuckled. "Don't look at me like that. I'm not feeding you lines. I want you to understand. I was caught off guard just the same way you were when I saw you again. You've had a chance to get used to the fact that the guy from the elevator is the same guy you need to talk to. I'm only just processing the fact that the hot chick I met in Dressel's building is someone I also need to take seriously."

She frowned at him. "You're going to take me seriously?"

He nodded solemnly. "Very seriously."

She looked suspicious. "In what way?"

He had to laugh. "I know what you're thinking, and you're right, but only partly right."

"What am I thinking?"

"That I mean I'm going to take fucking you very seriously. That I'm going to be very thorough about it."

She pursed her lips.

"That was what you thought, wasn't it?"

She nodded reluctantly.

"But I'm also taking you seriously about the lot and the community center. Do you want to know why I'm opening a second nightclub?"

"It's your business, and you're successful, so you're expanding."

He shook his head sadly.

"What then?"

"I'm opening a second nightclub because I'm bored shitless. I need a new challenge, and nothing else has presented itself yet."

"Wow."

It wasn't an impressed wow. In fact, she looked pretty disgusted, and he could understand why. "What?"

She shook her head. "It just seems crazy to me that you're bored, so you can go ahead and open a new nightclub, and in the process take away the one place that dozens of people rely on."

He nodded. "The world isn't fair, is it?"

She let out a short bitter laugh. "I was going to say you can say that again, but you really can. It's just words to you."

"I know. I've never experienced what those people have. I never will. But that doesn't make me an asshole."

She held his gaze for a moment, then nodded. "No, I don't suppose it does."

"I'd like to help. You're right, though. If I don't buy that lot, someone else will."

She downed the rest of her bourbon and got to her feet. "Thanks for your time, then."

Oscar stood to join her. "Where are you going? I didn't say I'm not going to help, did I?"

"No." The anger disappeared from her face, and in its place, there was confusion.

Oscar stepped closer. He didn't mean to; he couldn't help it. There was some force that pulled him toward her. He brushed a strand of hair away from her face, drawing a gasp from her lips and sending shockwaves through his body. "What do you want me to do?"

She looked up into his eyes, her full, pink lips were parted, and her breath was coming low and shallow. As soon as he realized she'd misunderstood the question, he was desperate to know what her answer might be.

"I want you to do all kinds of things. I want to do all kinds of things to you." She ran her tongue over her lips to moisten them, and the ache in his pants intensified. She drew in a deep breath. "What I don't want to do is confuse matters. I've come to you for help. I don't want to try to persuade you with sex."

His lips quirked. "Why not? It'd no doubt work."

She chuckled. "Or at least I could have fun trying, right?"

He nodded eagerly, but she shook her head. "No. I couldn't live with myself if I screwed you into helping out."

He nodded sadly. "Much as I'd love to argue with you, I can't. It'd work. I'm not denying that, but it'd screw everything else up, too."

"What else is there?"

He slid his arms around her waist and drew her to him. She didn't resist, and he closed his eyes briefly as he ran his hands down her back and brought his hands to rest on her backside. She felt so damned good. "How about this." He couldn't help it; he kneaded her ass as he spoke. "There are two separate and unrelated issues here. First, you need assistance in figuring out how to rehouse your center, correct?"

She nodded, and he was pleased to see that her eyes were glazed with lust. She let out a long slow breath as he held her ass and pressed his hips against hers. He'd swear he could feel the heat between her legs, and his cock strained to get to it.

"So, we'll set up a meeting. We'll talk about it, figure out what we can do."

Her eyes widened, but the surprise didn't dispel the lust.

"And the second issue is that there's something going on between the two of us. The guy and the girl who met in the elevator—they've got unfinished business, right?"

She nodded again. "They do."

He lowered his head. She was shorter than he remembered, but she lifted her lips to meet his. He started out slowly, wanting to taste her and savor the softness, but something about her ignited him. He crushed her to his chest and claimed her mouth. Her arms came up around his shoulders as she kissed him back. Her kisses were as feisty as she was. Her fingers tangled in his hair and pulled his head back. She lowered her lips to his neck and nibbled hungrily. Damn. That was a move he used often, but he hadn't been on the receiving end before. His knees started to buckle, and he walked her back to the couch where they sank down, and their lips found each other again.

She broke away after a few minutes and lifted her head. "I thought we weren't going to do that."

He smiled. "I don't remember saying we weren't."

She sat up. "But … but … I don't want you to help the center so that you can sleep with me, and I don't want to sleep with you so that you'll help the center."

Oscar sat up beside her. "So, don't."

As he'd suspected, there was disappointment in her eyes. What he hadn't expected was that it made him happy.

"Okay." She visibly pulled herself together. "I won't."

"Good. I'm glad we got that straight. And now we both understand each other, you can sleep with me just because you want to."

She met his gaze and held it for a long moment. He could see the struggle in her eyes. He held his breath wondering if she'd surrender or tell him to go screw himself. Eventually, she laughed. He loved the sound of it. It was genuine, real— something women rarely did around him.

He smiled. "Is that a yes?"

She nodded and put a hand on his shoulder drawing him in close. Finally. He'd met her a week ago, she'd invaded his

every waking moment since—and most of his dreams, too.
It'd been a long time since he'd had to wait this long to get
into a woman's panties. His eyelids lowered, and he leaned in
to brush her lips with his. He brushed thin air and opened his
eyes. She was smiling at him. "It's a yes, but not on a first
date."
He sat up straight. Was she screwing with him? "This isn't a
date."
"I know."

~ ~ ~

Grace's heart was hammering in her chest. What was she
doing? He wanted to screw her; she wanted to screw him. Why
was she doing this? She should just close her mouth and open
her legs. It'd be so easy! All the fantasizing she'd done since
she'd first set eyes on him could play out for real, right here on
his sofa or in his bed, on the floor, or wherever. It didn't
matter. The point was, she could be stripping off his clothes
right now, and he could be stripping off hers. Instead, she was
saying no, or at least, yes, but not yet? She must have finally
flipped.
She watched his face, wondering again if he was going to be
angry.
He wasn't. The corners of his lips turned up in that quirky
little smile. He brought his hand up to his mouth and ran his
thumb over his lips. She didn't know if he was trying to hide
his smile or drive her wild. He was succeeding at the latter.
"Are you saying we have to go on a date first?"
She pursed her lips. She didn't really know what she'd meant,
other than she wasn't going to have sex with him right now.
She shrugged. She knew men well enough to know that when
you don't answer them, they come up with what they think
you might mean. She'd see what he came up with and decide if
it suited her.

"Okay, so we go out on a date. Tomorrow night."

She smiled. She hadn't expected that.

He smiled back. "And since you aren't going to sleep with me on a first date, then we go out again on Saturday night."

"We can't."

His smile faded. "Why?"

"Because it's Saturday night. You're always at Six on Saturday night."

"Yes, so you can come there."

"That wouldn't be a date."

He narrowed his eyes and tried to hide a smile. "Okay, so Sunday. On Sunday, you're mine."

Her heart raced at the way he said it. Shivers ran down her spine, and her insides tingled in anticipation.

"Do you agree?"

She nodded slowly.

He held out his hand, and she shook it. They were sealing the deal, so why did it feel like she was sealing her fate?

He kept hold of her hand and drew her closer. She leaned in. Just because she wasn't going to have sex with him, didn't mean she couldn't kiss him some more. He claimed her mouth and kissed her more deeply than he had before. Keeping hold of her hand, he placed it over his erection, and she moaned. He was so hard and hot—and so big. He closed his arms around her and pulled her up into his lap, so she was straddling him. His lips never left hers, and she moaned into his mouth as he thrust up. She rocked her hips, loving the feel of his hardness pressing into her heat. She wished she'd worn a skirt, but knew that if she had, her protests about not on a first date wouldn't save her—from herself, let alone from Oscar.

After what felt like hours, his kissing slowed. Grace felt as though she was slowly returning to earth. She braced her hands on the sofa behind his head and pushed up, intending to sit back, but he tightened his arms around her and held her close, crushed to his chest. His kisses had slowed, but they were deepening, no less intense—if anything, more so. He was taking his time, exploring her mouth with his tongue while his hands explored her back and her ass. They too had slowed. Where before the passion between them had been fiery, this was something different. This was more … what? Intimate. She tensed at the realization. This wasn't just physical anymore. He was getting to know her, and it wasn't one-sided. She was getting to know him.

He ran his hands up to her shoulders and did the last thing she'd expected. He lifted his head with a smile, and he hugged her. He held her close, rested his head on her shoulder and hugged her. She wanted to swipe at the ridiculous stinging behind her eyes, but she didn't. She remained with her hands braced firmly against the sofa. She wanted to wait it out. It was crazy—the kind of emotional reaction a hug could elicit, but it was okay, she was immune to it. At least, she always had been. He continued to hold her like that until she started to relax. She could feel it, a kind of warmth that seeped through her. She couldn't resist it. Slowly she lifted her hands from the back of the sofa and wrapped her arms around his neck. She leaned her head against his and sighed. She didn't mean to; it was something that stirred deep within her and escaped her lips. Tears filled her eyes, but she had no idea why. She wasn't sad or angry or even frustrated. He nuzzled his lips into her neck, and she smiled. No, she wasn't any of those things; it was something crazier than that. She named it as she recognized it—she was happy.

"You're an unusual lady, Grace."

She chuckled. "I'm not sure I want to know what that means."

He leaned his head back against the sofa and looked up into her eyes. "I'm not sure I can tell you. I will say that you do things to me."

She rocked her hips and closed her eyes against the feel of his hard cock and the ripples of pleasure it sent coursing through her.

He pursed his lips. "Yes. That. But that's what I was looking for. That's what I wanted and expected." He closed his arms around her again and hugged her. "This," he murmured. "The way this makes me feel. This is what I didn't expect. What I didn't think a woman could do to me, or for me."

She nuzzled into his neck. She wasn't sure she liked what this feeling meant, but she did know she enjoyed it. "I sure as hell didn't expect it."

He looked up at her with a smile. "You feel it, too?"

She nodded. "I'd love to lie. I'd love to run a mile and deny it, but I can't. You're being honest with me. I owe you the same."

He grinned. "I guess all we can do is enjoy it."

"I guess." She wasn't stupid. She'd enjoy it while it lasted, but she didn't expect that to be very long. She slid down from his lap. She was fairly certain she'd see him tomorrow night, and then on Sunday. He'd keep feeling it until she slept with him, but it wouldn't go any further than that. She picked up her glass and drained the last of the bourbon. Even if she did allow herself to enjoy his company, and that feeling—the intimacy—she couldn't get off track. It was all about the center.

"So, Miss ... Grace. Are you going to tell me your last name, by the way? When would be a good time for you to meet to talk about your community center, and what I can do to help?"

She wanted to hug him again. It was as if he'd read her mind. "Whenever suits you. You're the one with the busy schedule."

"I'm guessing you're working tomorrow, and I know you have a hot date tomorrow night." He winked.

Part of her still wanted to think of him as an arrogant prick, but she couldn't. It was just so damned sexy, and she was starting to feel that there might be a whole lot more to him than just arrogance. "That's right."

He smirked. "And you're busy Saturday night."

"I am?"

He nodded. "You are. Apparently, it doesn't count as a date because it's at my place of work, but you're still going out with me on Saturday night."

He was an arrogant prick! But she didn't want to say no. "Okay."

"So, what are you doing on Saturday afternoon?"

"It sounds like I'm meeting with you. And it's Evans."

"Okay, Grace Evans. Will I be welcome at this center of yours? Do you want to meet there, so you can show me around?"

Wow. She hadn't expected that. "Yes."

"Great." He smiled. "I have you all tied up till Monday, then."

Grace smiled. "It looks that way."

Chapter Nine

Oscar stared at his computer screen. He wasn't seeing it, though. He couldn't focus. All he could think about was Grace. He kept trying to convince himself that it was nothing more than a serious case of blue balls. When he'd gone to meet her last night, he'd have put money on the fact that he was going to screw her. But no. That hadn't panned out. He'd see her again tonight, even though he already knew she wasn't going to give in. He smiled to himself. He hadn't lied when he told her she was an unusual woman. She was a rare bird indeed. In fact, she might be unique. At least, insofar as he didn't think he'd ever been on a date before that he didn't believe had fairly good odds of him getting laid.

So why was he so looking forward to it? Maybe it was because he had to get the first date out of the way in order to get to the second one—the one where the odds of getting her into bed rose dramatically. Then again, maybe it wasn't just that. In fact, he knew it wasn't. He was looking forward to this evening for its own sake. He was looking forward to seeing her, spending time with her, talking to her, getting to know her and who she was. He shook his head. If he couldn't focus on work, maybe he should see what he could find out about her.

He searched the address of the lot on Gascoigne Street and frowned. There were no results about a community center. Nothing at all. He pursed his lips, and his heart beat faster. Was she some kind of con artist? Damn, he hoped not. He searched for her name, but the only thing he found was a line on Dressel, CPA's one-page website, listing Grace Evans as Office Manager, whatever that meant. There were a couple of social media profiles, but none of them were her. He didn't like it. In this day and age, everyone left a footprint online. How and why would one woman and her community center be such a mystery—unless they didn't exist?

He pushed his chair back from his desk and left the office. "TJ?"

His brother popped his head out of the security office. "In here. What's up? Do you need a ride?"

Oscar nodded as he strode down the hallway toward the back entrance. "Yeah."

"Is something wrong?" TJ asked as they got into the limo.

Oscar shrugged as he closed the passenger door and fastened his seat belt. "I don't know, but I don't like it. I've got a bad feeling."

"About what?" TJ started the car and turned to him. "Now I've got a bad feeling, too, and I don't even know what you're talking about."

Oscar gave him a rueful smile. "I'm not sure I want you to. I might just be being paranoid."

"Just because you're paranoid, doesn't mean they're not out to get you," said TJ with a smile. "Where are we going? You can tell me all about it on the way."

"We're going to the lot on Gascoigne Street."

"Okay." TJ pulled out of the lot. "What do you think you're paranoid about?"

"Can I reserve judgment till we've been over there?"

"If you want to." TJ drove on in silence for a few minutes.

"Okay. I'll tell you."

TJ hadn't spoken another word, but the question was hanging in the air between them. "I saw Grace last night."

"Office girl?"

"Yep and the reason she came looking for me was because she runs a community center in the building on the lot."

"And you didn't know this?"

"I had no clue. All I knew was that I'm buying based on the value of the land. The building was listed as being of no market value. I figured it'd need tearing down. I had no clue that it's a meeting place for people."

"What kind of people?"

"From what she said, kids and single moms and vets."

TJ's eyes widened at that. "Homeless vets?"

Of course, that'd be what TJ picked up on. "I assume so."

TJ kept his gaze on the traffic ahead. "And you've known all this since last night, but what made you want to go over there now?"

"I googled her. I searched to see what I could find out about the center and about her. And I can't find anything."

"Nothing?"

"Nothing at all. Don't you think it's strange that a community center wouldn't have a website, wouldn't be mentioned in news articles?"

"Not necessarily. Sometimes, places like that are all about word of mouth. It's not like you can just crack open your laptop to check out the blogs when you're living under the bridge."

Oscar pursed his lips. He wanted to argue, but he knew that homelessness and in particular the way vets were treated, was a trigger point for TJ.

"Even if the center doesn't show up in any searches, don't you think it's strange that Grace doesn't either?"

TJ chuckled. "You've been on one date, and now you're stalking her on the web?"

"No." Oscar ran his hand through his hair. "I'm not stalking her. I just wanted to check her out, but there's nothing to check."

"You think she gave you the wrong name?"

"I don't know. I don't know what to think."

"But you're going over there to confront her, to find out?"

"Honestly? I don't know what the hell I'm doing. I want to see if this center even exists. Which now I've calmed down a little may be dumb, considering she invited me to see it tomorrow, said she'd show me around."

"At least you can drop in on her, surprise her."

Oscar shook his head. "No. She doesn't work there. She works for Dressel, the guy I'm buying the lot from."

"Okay, so maybe you can just stop in, look around, get a feel for the place?"

"I suppose." He'd set out fueled by suspicion. He wasn't about to get conned somehow, but with a little time to reflect, he realized that that wasn't very likely. Grace must have some reason for keeping a low to non-existent profile online, but he seriously doubted that she was a con artist. He looked over at TJ. "What are you smirking about?"

"Nothing. I was just thinking that if this was some kind of hustle, she'd probably have made sure that there was a website and all kinds of evidence online to back her up."

Oscar nodded.

When they pulled up in front of the lot, Oscar stared out the window at the building. He'd seen it in the photographs, but he hadn't been down here himself until now. He hadn't needed to. His appraiser had been over. He'd focused on the lot itself and the supporting infrastructure. Oscar had been more concerned about whether the existing utilities could support a new commercial venture. It hadn't occurred to him that they might already be supporting a charitable one.

"What do you want to do? Are you going in?"

Oscar shrugged. Grace was supposed to bring him here tomorrow. He didn't know what to expect if he walked in there now. He couldn't imagine he'd be too popular with whoever was inside. He was the guy who was about to take their building away.

"This girl must be really getting to you. Are you telling me you don't know what to do?"

Oscar shrugged again. He couldn't believe it either.

TJ unfastened his seat belt.

"What are you doing?"

"I'm going in there myself. I'll have a look around. Ask about the vets programs."

Oscar nodded. "That makes sense. Thanks, TJ." He shook his head as he watched his brother walk inside the run-down building. What was this Grace doing to him? First, he'd gotten paranoid, and now he was letting his brother do his dirty work for him. None of this was like him. He didn't do paranoia, he didn't need to—he relied on his instincts, and they never steered him wrong. And he didn't rely on anyone; he didn't need to do that either. Maybe this was a good thing? Relying on his brother's help could be good for both of them.

He stared out through the window of the limo and waited, trying not to think about how much the girl with the long dark hair—and the great ass—was getting to him.

~ ~ ~

"Are you sure you don't want me to do your makeup?" asked Louise.

Grace shook her head adamantly. "This is a date. If he wants to go out with me, then he should see who I really am."

"I know, and you're beautiful, but ..."

Grace laughed. "Thanks for the vote of confidence, but ... what?"

"I don't mean it like that. I just meant he's used to going out with celebrities, models. He's used to made up perfection."

"Exactly. If that's what he wants, he's barking up the wrong tree with me, and the sooner we both figure that out, the better. Don't you think?"

Louise nodded reluctantly. "I forget how empowered you are."

Grace had to laugh. "You keep saying that word about me. I'm just realistic. I don't want to live a lie. I'm not going to try to be someone else or look like someone else just so he'll like me. If he likes me for me, that'll be awesome. If not, fair enough. That won't bother me. Not everyone's going to like me, and I don't expect them to, but if I'm going to spend some time with a guy, then I want it to be because he likes me, not because he likes some image I'm trying to portray."

Louise nodded. "I know, you're right, you're just so much braver than I am. I'd be getting all dolled up trying to please him."

Grace sighed. "Maybe you're right. I mean, it's not like it's going to go anywhere. It's going to be a couple of dates and wham, bam, thank you, ma'am. I'm under no illusions. It's just a glorified one-night stand." She chuckled. "I suppose it's a one-weekend stand."

"I wouldn't knock it if I were you. A lot of girls would give anything for a one-night stand with Oscar Davenport."

"I know, but I'm not like a lot of girls." Grace smiled remembering the way he'd told her she was an unusual lady.

"Just look at that smile," said Louise.

"Whatever." Grace stood back to check herself out in the mirror. They were going to dinner. She didn't know where; he hadn't told her. She'd insisted she didn't want to go anywhere too fancy. Louise thought she was afraid of feeling out of place, but that wasn't it at all. Grace just couldn't stand the thought of spending ridiculous amounts of money on one meal for two people—not when she knew how many people could be fed for less.

She looked good. The skirt might be a bad idea—a very bad idea if he wanted to slide his hand up her thigh like he had in the club. She wouldn't be able to turn him down if he wanted to persuade her that way. He'd already warned her he could be very persuasive—and part of her would love to find out. She sighed. She'd find out soon enough—on Sunday to be precise. If she didn't succumb and climb all over him before that. If she could keep a lid on it, they'd have dinner tonight, she'd show him around the center tomorrow, and then tomorrow night they'd have an evening at the club. Sunday would be soon enough to sleep with him, even though she had a nasty suspicion that it would feel like way too soon to say goodbye.

"I think he's here," Louise called from Grace's bedroom where she'd gone to look out the window.

Grace went in and knelt on the bed beside her. "Yep."

Louise almost had her nose up against the glass. "He's sitting up front."

"Yeah."

"Oh my God, Grace. Look at the driver!"

"What about him?" Grace knew he was a big guy, she'd seen him last night. She peered down at the street. "Oh." That wasn't the guy who'd been driving last night. He was hot! He looked a lot like Oscar, except a little fairer.

"Oh, Gracie! Can I come? I'll keep the driver busy while you and Oscar have dinner."

Grace laughed. "I don't think so."

Louise let herself fall back onto the bed. "He's gorgeous! We could keep the back seat warm for you."

Grace laughed. "No, thanks."

"Can you get his number for me?"

"No."

"Please? He's my dream guy, my every fantasy come true. Tell him you have a roommate who could make any fantasy he likes come true."

"Louise!" Grace shook her head disapprovingly. "Have a little self-respect. Just because he's good-looking …"

"What?"

"You shouldn't want to make all his fantasies come true. He might want to do anything."

Louise laughed. "That's kind of my point. I'd like to do anything he can think of. I can feel my uterus contract just looking at him. He's swoon worthy." She'd scrambled back up and was staring out the window at him.

"I'd better go." Grace looked around for her purse.

"Let me walk you out."

Grace laughed. "Only if you come right now. I'm not waiting while you fix your makeup."

Louise smiled sweetly and pulled a lipstick out of her pocket. "No, problem. After you." She opened the door and let Grace go out ahead of her. "You're not nervous, are you?" she asked as they made their way down the stairs.

"No. I'm not."

"I would be. I'm nervous about meeting the driver."

"You're not going to meet him. You can just peek at him."

Louise grinned and let them out through the front door. "We'll see about that."

Grace watched Oscar step out of the car, and her heart started to pound. It wasn't nerves. It was just something about the man. She'd reacted to him that way the first time she'd seen him get out of the limo in front of Harry's office, and the effect hadn't worn off.

"You're so lucky!" whispered Louise.

"He's the lucky one." Grace tried to sound like she meant it, but watching Oscar stride toward them, that sexy, cocky smile on his face, she had to agree with her friend.

"Grace." He slid his arm around her waist and leaned down to peck her cheek. It was a casual gesture, the kind of thing friends did all the time, but it rendered her speechless. She'd spent much of today wondering if she'd merely imagined that sense of intimacy between them last night. One little peck on the cheek told her she hadn't. The force that drew them together was still strong.

Since she couldn't seem to muster any words, Oscar smiled at Louise. "Oscar Davenport. It's nice to meet you. You must be Louise."

Louise smiled and babbled at him. Grace looked on, trying to remember when she'd told him about Louise. She glanced over at the limo and caught the driver watching them intently. It made her shudder. Louise was chattering away, telling Oscar to have fun, but be good. Grace caught his eye, and he smirked.

"Can we give you a ride?"

Grace managed not to groan out loud, but she rolled her eyes.

"Oh, no. I wouldn't want to impose, or take you out of your way."

"It's not a problem, is it, Grace? We need to go, our reservation is at eight, but TJ can drop us off first and then take you wherever you want to go."

Grace had to bite back a laugh. That sounded like Louise's fantasies coming true.

"Thank you!" Louise trotted around to the passenger door. "I should sit up front though and let you two get on with your date."

Before anyone could argue, she'd opened the door and sat beside the driver. He looked a little startled, but Louise launched straight into her friendly, ditzy, flirting.

Oscar smiled at Grace. "You don't mind?"

"I don't, but you probably should have asked TJ first; he's the one who's going to have a problem getting rid of her."

"Ah." Oscar peered in through driver's window, but TJ was turned toward Louise, smiling and nodding here and there as she chattered away.

When they were seated in the back, Oscar pressed the button, and the little window slid open.

"Everything okay?" asked TJ.

"I hope so." Oscar winked at Grace. "Would you mind dropping us off first? We're cutting it fine to get there on time."

Grace was surprised by the look TJ gave Oscar in the rearview mirror. They must be close, she wouldn't have thought a driver would get away with glaring at his employer like that. Oscar made a face back at him—at least it all seemed good-natured.

Grace managed to catch TJ's eye and mouthed sorry. She was shocked when he grinned back—and winked!

Chapter Ten

Oscar watched Grace's face with amusement when TJ brought the limo to a halt. She stared out the window at Gavin's Place looking deeply perplexed.

"Here you go, guys. Have fun." TJ had turned around in his seat so he could talk through the window to them.

Grace looked at him, then at Oscar. "This is where we're going?"

"Yeah. Is this okay?"

"Of course." She made to open the door, but TJ was out and came around to open it for her before she could.

"Bye, Louise," Oscar said, then got out and went around to join his brother and Grace.

They all stood there for a moment. Grace seemed to have recovered, but TJ was giving him an evil look.

"I'm sorry about Louise." Grace gave TJ an apologetic smile. "She's a good person, just a little enthusiastic."

TJ smiled graciously. "It's not a problem. I'll take her wherever she wants to go." He turned to Oscar. "Do you want to call me and let me know when you're ready?"

"Yeah, thanks." He smirked. "But if you get busy first, just let me know. We can take a cab."

"There's no need." He turned to Grace. "Have a good time, and don't take any crap from him." With that, he got back in the limo and pulled away.

Grace gave Oscar a puzzled look.

"What?"

"I don't know what I'm more surprised by. The way TJ talks to you, or the fact that we're here."

He smiled. "How about we go in, and I'll tell you about TJ?"

"Okay."

He opened the door for her and let her go inside ahead of him. Gavin's Place was a run-down neighborhood bar and diner. She'd insisted she didn't want to go anywhere fancy, and he'd complied. He was curious what she'd make of this, and he was about to find out.

It was dark inside, and there were only a few tables occupied. Grace made her way to an empty booth in the back and raised an eyebrow at him. "Is this okay?"

He nodded, wondering why she seemed irritated.

Once they were seated, she picked a menu out of the rack and started to study it.

"Is everything okay?"

"Yeah." She looked up.

"It's obviously not. Are you going to tell me what's wrong? If you don't like it here ..."

"I love it here. I'm just surprised at you. I know I said I didn't want to go anywhere fancy, but you didn't need to pick a dive where you no doubt wouldn't ever go otherwise."

He tried to hide a smile as he saw Gavin come out from behind the bar and amble over to their table.

"Evening Oscar. You want a Coors?"

"Yeah, thanks, Gavin."

Grace looked confused but recovered quickly as Gavin smiled at her. "What about you, love?"

"I'll take a Coors, too, thanks."

"Coming right up. Do you need a minute with that?" He jerked his chin at the menu in Grace's hand.

"Yes."

"Okay. I'm guessing I already know what you want, right?"

Oscar grinned. "Yep, the usual, please."

When he'd gone, Grace scowled at him. "Okay, so I just made a fool of myself, assuming you wouldn't normally come in here. Do you want to tell me what's going on?"

"I will but decide what you want to eat first. Gavin doesn't mess around. He'll be back in under two minutes with our drinks, and he'll want to know."

She looked back down at the menu and nodded. "Okay."

Gavin proved Oscar right and returned with two iced beer mugs. "You decided?"

"Yep, I'll have the meatloaf, thanks."

Gavin smiled. "He's right. It is good. Two orders of meatloaf coming up."

Oscar chuckled as he walked away. "It's not just good; it's amazing."

Grace shook her head.

"What, you're surprised that's what I eat in here?"

"Yeah. I am. You're full of surprises, aren't you?"

"Am I? Like what?"

She smirked. "Let's see. First of all, I expect you to feel out of place in a dive like this, but you're right at home. Then, you drink beer instead of bourbon or even wine. And now you're telling me that meatloaf is your favorite."

He shrugged. "It's only my favorite here. Gavin makes it just like my mom does. It's like getting a taste of home." He'd hoped that talking about Mom's meatloaf might relax her a little—make her see him as a bit more normal, and not just Oscar Davenport, the billionaire. Apparently, it wasn't working. Instead of her opening up, it seemed like she'd shut down on him. "From your reaction, I'd guess you don't like meatloaf, but you just ordered it. So, it can't be that. Did I say something wrong?"

"No. I can imagine that line would work with a lot of women. Your intention was to disarm and make a connection, right?"

He nodded. He wasn't used to women being so blunt. "That was the intention, yes, but it didn't work, did it? Want to tell me why?"

She shrugged. "I don't really want to, no, but I will."

He waited as she took a sip of her beer.

"I ordered the meatloaf because it's comfort food to me, too, but for a very different reason."

"Your mom makes terrible meatloaf?" he ventured, hoping to get a smile. It didn't work.

"I wouldn't know. I don't even know if she's still alive."

"Oh." Oscar had nothing, so he waited.

She gave him a wry smile. "Don't look like that. I'm not feeling sorry for myself or looking for pity. It was just a timely reminder of how different we are."

"Are we?" He didn't believe that was true. They might come from different backgrounds, have different circumstances, but Oscar felt her to be some kind of kindred spirit. A thought that surprised the hell out of him.

She laughed. "Just totally."

"How so?"

"Oh, come on. You have a mom who still makes you meatloaf. I had a mom who rarely fed us, even before she left us."

"What about your dad?"

"He died when I was a few months old."

"And your mom left you?"

She blew out a sigh. "Yeah. She kept us together for a while, but eventually, the drugs and the booze and the boyfriends won."

Oscar's heart hammered in his chest, and not in the way it usually did around her. "What happened?"

"Child Services took me and my sister and two brothers and put us in the system."

"The system?"

"Yeah, the foster care system. There are some wonderful people with big hearts and great intentions in that system." She pursed her lips and stared into space for a moment, before adding. "Unfortunately for me, I never met any of them."

Oscar shook his head. "I'm sorry."

She smiled. "It's not your fault. It's just the way it is. I turned out all right." She gave him the first genuine smile since they'd come in here. "They say the system builds character."

He smiled. "I'd have to agree with that in your case."

~ ~ ~

Grace stared at him, wondering why she was opening up to him like this. It hadn't been her plan, but he'd caught her off guard, and she was too good at telling the truth.

"Anyway, my story's nothing special. I'm not alone." She smiled. "You'll meet a bunch of kids tomorrow who are living the same life I did." Oscar nodded. She didn't want him to clam up and sure as hell didn't want him feeling sorry for her.

"What about you? Where did you grow up? I see you as coming from a big, loving family, especially with the mention of your mom's meatloaf. Are you close to your folks?"

He nodded. "I am close to them. They're good people, and I know how fortunate I am." He pursed his lips. "Part of me doesn't want to let you change the subject this easily. I want to know more about you, but," he smiled, "I did tell you I'd explain about TJ."

"He's your brother!"

Oscar grinned. "Yep."

"The poor guy. He'll probably need rescuing from Louise. She got so excited when she looked out the window and saw him. I thought he kind of looked like you."

"I guess he does, but I'm the good-looking one."

She laughed. "You really are an arrogant prick, aren't you?"

He laughed with her. "I prefer to say confident, but yeah, you're not the first to tell me that."

Grace nodded, the laughter drying up in her throat. For a moment there, she'd been relaxed, just enjoying a date with a guy, but his words reminded her. He wasn't just a guy. This wasn't going to be a date that led to some boyfriend and girlfriend type thing. He was rich and good-looking and had women lining up waiting for their turn in his bed. It reminded her that nothing she said would be something he hadn't heard a dozen times before from other women.

He gave her a puzzled look, but Gavin saved her from having to explain by returning with their food. "Here you go. Enjoy."

"Is TJ your only brother?" she asked as soon as Gavin had gone.

Oscar met her gaze. "I take it that means you don't want to explain how I upset you?"

"You didn't upset me."

He gave her a knowing look.

"Okay, let's leave it at you take it right. I don't want to explain. So, is he?"

He held her gaze for a moment longer, and she was grateful when he chose not to pursue it. "No. There are three of us. I'm the eldest, then TJ, then Reid."

Grace nodded. "And TJ works for you?"

"No. Not really. He's driving for me at the moment, but ..."

"I don't mean to pry."

"He was Special Forces. He had a rough go on his last deployment. He was at something of a loss when he came back. This is kind of a stepping-stone for him. Driving for me gives him some purpose without too much pressure."

"He's lucky."

"I feel like I'm the lucky one, that I can help out."

Grace bit the inside of her lip. She wanted to tell him that he could get really lucky if he wanted to help a whole bunch of vets with similar stories to TJ's but without the same resources. She wanted to, and she would, but she'd save it for tomorrow. "You are."

"Do you have family in the military?"

"Not that I know of. Why?"

"Your reaction; it made it seem like it hit close to home."

"It does." She smiled. "I wanted to tell you about some of the guys at the center, but it can wait."

"Till tomorrow?"

"Yeah. And what about Reid?"

Oscar smiled. "Reid does his own thing. If I'm the suit, and TJ's the uniform, then Reid would be the geek."

Grace smiled. "You love them, don't you?"

"I do."

She loved that he wasn't shy about it.

"I know how fortunate I am, and I don't just mean that I come from a wealthy family. I mean that I come from a great family. My parents are awesome people, and so are my brothers."

"And your cousin is an amazing lady, too, from what I understand."

"You know Hope?"

She laughed. "Not personally, of course, but I remember her as a model, and she's done a lot of charity work."

"She has, and so have I."

Grace laughed. "What, you don't want to be outdone in the good works department?"

"No, I don't. You already think I'm an arrogant prick. I want you to know there's more to me than the sexy playboy."

She shook her head. "So modest. What charity work do you do?"

She was surprised how eagerly he leaned forward. "All kinds. Have you heard of Clay McAdam?"

"Err, yeah. I don't even like country music, but I don't live under a rock. Of course, I've heard of him. Don't tell me you've helped him with the kids' charity?"

"I helped him set it up. We did a big concert to kick everything off. I'm still on the board."

Grace put her fork down and sat back. "You're on the board?"

"I am. Does that surprise you?"

She shrugged, not wanting to admit just how much it surprised her.

"That's okay. People tend to assume that donations are the extent of my involvement. And I don't need to shout about it."

"Except to me."

Her heart fluttered as he cocked his head to one side and gave her a boyish smile. "Of course. I'm going to shout about it to you. It's something that's important to you, and I'm trying to make a good impression here. Give a guy a break?"

She laughed. It was hard to believe that he was out to make a good impression on her, but she liked it. A lot. She held his gaze, and they both smiled. That warm feeling crept through her again, as though they were making some kind of connection that went beyond words. She sat up straight as Gavin came back. She needed to get a grip.

"More beer?"

"Yes, please." She smiled at Gavin as he took her mug and he smiled back.

"You can bring her in here again," he told Oscar.

Grace gave him a puzzled look, but he just laughed. "Thanks, Gavin."

They ate in silence for a few minutes until Gavin returned with fresh beers. "I didn't put my foot in it, did I?"

"No," said Oscar with a smile.

"Maybe," said Grace. "What did you mean?"

Gavin held his hands up and shook his head. "I'll let his lordship explain."

Grace looked at Oscar expectantly. "Well?"

He gave her a beseeching look. "Don't get mad at me?"

"I might. I might not. Try me."

He blew out a sigh. "I don't know what it is about you, but I can't bullshit you."

She laughed. "I'm not going to get mad about that."

"Okay. I've been coming in here for years. The first time I came was when ... to escape ..."

Grace chuckled. "Let me guess, you had some chick stalking you everywhere you went, so you couldn't go to any of your usual places?"

"Yes. And I discovered the meatloaf and started coming back. This has become my comfort place for comfort food. I brought a date here once, and it was a total disaster. I asked Gavin to kick my ass for me if I ever brought a woman here again—and I haven't."

"But you brought me."

"I did."

"Because I fit in here?"

His smile faded. "Yes and no. Not in the way I think you mean."

"What that it's a divey neighborhood bar and I'm a divey neighborhood kind of girl?"

He scowled. "Definitely not that. If that's what you think, that's your problem, and it's not how I see you."

She bit back a smile. She liked that he was getting mad at her on her behalf. Spider was the only person who did that.

"I meant you fit in, because ... I don't know how to explain it. This is my comfort place, and you're ... comfortable to be with."

She raised her eyebrows, and he grimaced.

"Don't look like that. Comfort is a good thing. I don't usually feel comfortable around people. I ..."

She laughed. "Quit while you're ahead. Or at least, stop digging. I take it as a compliment. I don't feel comfortable around people either."

"Are you comfortable with me?"

She thought about it. "Yeah, probably more than I should be."

It was true. He made her heart pound. She was anxious about what he might be prepared to do to help out at the center, but she was comfortable with him.

"What does that mean?" he looked puzzled.

"Just that I shouldn't get used to it."

"Why not?"

She rolled her eyes. "I thought you weren't going to bullshit me. We're going to hang out for a couple of days. You're going to decide what you might do to help the center. We both know we're delaying the inevitable when it comes to screwing each other's brains out. Beyond that …" She shrugged. "Well, that's where our paths will part again. I don't want to get comfortable being comfortable. Don't get me wrong, it's nice, but …" She shrugged again, feeling like she'd said too much.

He didn't argue. He just stared at her. Part of her wished he say something nice, disagree with her. Mostly she was grateful that he wasn't going to lie about it.

After Gavin had cleared their plates, she sat back and smiled at him.

"What?"

"Nothing."

"So, what are you looking so smug about?"

"I'm not. What you're mistaking for smugness is actually content."

"You're content?"

"Yeah. This has been fun. Not what I expected at all."

"You thought it wouldn't be fun?"

"Kind of. I thought it'd be tense. You know? We're so different, and there's the whole issue of the center and whether I'm just courting you for a donation." She waggled her eyebrows at him. "Not to mention the physical side. I thought there'd be some tension."

He chuckled. "You don't feel the tension? I thought it was coming off me in waves."

"I feel it, but it's not awkward. It's there, but it's not overbearing."

He gave her the sad, puppy dog eyes. "You're not overwhelmed with desire for me then?"

She had to laugh. "No."

"Damn."

He waved a hand at Gavin for the check. "So, I need to step up my game?"

She shook her head. "No. I didn't say there's no desire. I'm just not overwhelmed, and that's a good thing."

"It is?"

"Yeah. See, it gets overwhelming when that's all there is. I've been too busy enjoying your company to focus solely on the physical side."

He grinned. "Me too. I didn't realize it until you said it, but you're right. This has been like making a new friend."

"Instead of having to listen to a woman talk until you can get in her panties?"

That smile! If he'd wanted into her panties at that moment, she would have agreed. But he was right, she felt as though she was making a friend.

"Guilty as charged. That's usually me." His smile faded, and he looked puzzled. "I told you, Grace, you're an unusual lady."

"Thank you."

When he'd paid Gavin, they made their way out onto the street. He slung his arm around her shoulders, and she looked up into his eyes. Who would ever have guessed that Big Cat, the arrogant prick, would turn out to be a good guy?

"I want to walk with you for a while. I want to take you home. I want a lot of things, Grace. But most of all I want to honor our agreement. So, I'm going to call TJ and ask him to come get us and drop you home."

If he'd said he wanted her to go home with him, she would have gone—eagerly. Part of her was disappointed; part of her was glad that he wasn't only about having sex with her.

They both turned to look as the limo pulled up to the curb.

Oscar gave her a rueful smile. "There. Decision made for us. I was wavering, thinking I could call a cab to take us back to my place."

She wondered why TJ couldn't do just that.

As he'd already done a couple of times, Oscar seemed to read her mind. "I can't ask TJ to do that. I already asked him not to let me take you home."

"Why?"

He put his hands on her shoulders and looked down into her eyes. "Because I don't want to screw this up."

He lowered his head, and she lifted her lips to meet his. His kisses did strange things to her, not just the usual, expected, physical things—making her knees weak, and her head spin, and the heat build between her legs. No, he checked all those boxes. What was strange was that his kisses felt like coming home—only she'd never had a home.

Chapter Eleven

Grace sat at the counter in the coffee shop, stirring her coffee and staring into space.

"Do you know what you want from him?" Spider interrupted her daydreams.

She stared at him for a long moment. She'd just been thinking about what she wanted from Oscar, but she sure as hell wasn't going to tell Spider about it. In her imagination they'd just been lying on his sofa, they were down to their underwear, lips and limbs entangled, and she'd been very close to getting what she wanted. She shook her head. That wasn't what Spider was talking about. "I want to see what he's prepared to offer. I've been thinking about it a lot. I could ask for an amount of money—but whatever amount it was might be much more, or much less than he'd be willing to give. I could ask for something specific, but that would rule out any ideas he might come up with himself. He's a smart guy. He might have something in mind that hasn't occurred to us. So, I'm just going to wait and see."

Spider nodded. "That makes sense. What time is he supposed to be here?"

"Twelve-thirty." She couldn't wait to see him again. It had only been twelve hours since TJ had dropped her back at Louise's last night. She hadn't been able to sleep, tossing and turning—all hot and horny and wishing that he'd taken her home.

Spider checked his watch. "Not long then. Do you mind if I follow you over there? I'll give you some time to show him around and that, but I'd like to talk to him."

"Of course." Although she tended to oversee the decisions regarding the center, Spider did just as much for the place as she did. She wasn't trying to make this about her and what she wanted. It was about what would be best for everyone.

"Okay. I'll give you a half hour head start and then I'll come over."

"Is there anything that you want from him?"

Spider smiled. "I'll be happy if he wants to do anything at all, as far as the center goes. I also want to have a word with him about my girl."

"Your girl?"

"You, dumbass. You know what I mean."

"What?"

He shrugged. "I don't know, but I just want to remind him that you're not some poor damsel in distress. That just because you're coming to him for help, it doesn't mean he can take advantage of you."

Grace laughed. "You think I could be taken advantage of?"

"Not really, but you never know. I don't want him trying."

"What if I do?"

"If you do, that's your business, and it won't be my place to say a damned thing, not to you." He held her gaze for a long moment. "Do you?"

She nodded. "I'm going out with him again tonight and tomorrow."

"Fair enough. I knew you liked him. I won't lay it on too hard, then."

"Thanks."

~ ~ ~

Oscar pulled up outside the coffee shop. TJ had offered to drive him, but it was his day off, and Oscar had wanted the time to himself. He was trying to get his head straight. Grace had him all turned around. He wanted her more than he could remember wanting any woman, but then he couldn't remember having to wait this long to get a woman into bed either. He'd known her for ten days, and she still hadn't slept with him. He shook his head. It was about more than that, though. She was in the way of his plans, and that bothered him. Normally, he didn't let people get in the way. He sidelined them or sidestepped them—and occasionally bulldozed them if they were assholes.

He didn't want to sideline Grace. He didn't even want to work around her. Her agenda was more important to him than his own. He sat up and looked himself in the eye in the rearview mirror. Had he really just admitted that? Yep. He had. It wasn't that her agenda was more important because it was hers. It was more important because she was involved in something that was in line with his own values. She was doing something that mattered, something that made a difference in people's lives. He was just …what? Entertaining himself by providing entertainment for others. He blew out a sigh. So? Entertainment wasn't wrong. It was fun. Everyone needed fun in their lives—especially him. That was why he'd gotten into the club business. He'd needed fun after spending his time with stuffy bankers running the hedge fund.

Had he just had enough fun? Was one club already more than enough? He needed substance in his life too. He needed balance. He might do a bunch of charity work with Clay and a couple of other foundations, but it wasn't much. TJ had kept letting his disapproval be known since he'd been back. Oscar had kept telling him that he needed to find some balance in his life. He was so serious, so intense. He needed to learn to relax and laugh a little.

He peered through the windshield. He could see Grace sitting inside the coffee shop. She was at the counter talking to the big burly dude she'd introduced him to the other night. He should get in there. Get on with this. Figure out what they wanted from him. What he could do to help. And while he was at it, maybe he could figure out what he wanted out of life. She looked up when he pushed the door open. Damn, she was beautiful. She was wearing a black top and those weird, but wonderful purple tights. He was more used to women in designer dresses, women with perfect hair and makeup, but none of them could hold a candle to her. She was fresh; she was real; she was doing a number on him, and he was powerless to resist. He smiled back, holding her gaze as he approached the counter.

"Davenport." He finally tore his eyes away from her at the sound of her friend's voice.

Spider. That was what she'd called him. Oscar nodded. He liked the guy. He wouldn't want to piss him off, but he liked him. "Spider. It's good to see you again."

Spider nodded. "You, too. I hope your visit to the center will give you an idea of what we do—of what people are going to lose when you tear the place down and open your new club."

Oscar nodded. He wasn't going to get into any kind of confrontation—especially since he didn't know if there'd be any reason for it.

Grace shot Spider a look that clearly told him to back off. Oscar was surprised when the guy smiled. "Hey, it's no secret what's going on here, is it?"

Oscar smiled back. "I don't suppose it is. I want to help; I do. I just need to get an idea of what the center's all about. What you're going to need."

"Why don't we head over there, then?" Grace offered.

"Are you coming?" Oscar met Spider's gaze. He didn't know what Grace might have told him about the two of them, but the guy wasn't stupid. Oscar wanted to include him and to get his take on the center. Grace had said he played a big brother role in her life and getting him on his side wouldn't do any harm.

"Yeah. You two go on, and I'll catch up with you in a little while."

"Okay. We'll see you over there."

When they reached the car, Oscar opened the door for Grace to slide into the passenger side. When he slid into the driver's seat, she greeted him with a smile.

He turned to face her. "Hi."

"Hey."

"I want to lean over there and kiss you. I've been looking forward to it ever since I let you go last night."

Her smile grew bigger. "So, why don't you?"

He did. He leaned across and slid his hand into her hair, pulling her closer so he could taste the plump pink lips that featured in so many of his fantasies lately. She kissed him back, gripping his shoulders and pulling him to her.

When they finally came up for air, he held her gaze. For a moment, the pull of her was still so strong. He hadn't been lying last night when he'd said he felt like he was making a new friend. He felt so close to her; she wasn't just a hot body, a pretty face, or a physical pleasure he was chasing. She was so much more than that. He didn't know what to do with it. It seemed she didn't either. He could see so many questions in her eyes, then they were gone, and she smiled. "We should probably get out of here. I don't think Spider would approve if he comes out and finds us making out."

Oscar shot a glance over his shoulder at the coffee shop. He felt a momentary flash of defiance. Grace was his girl, and if they wanted to kiss in the car, they would. No one could stop them. When the thought faded, he was surprised at himself. For starters, she wasn't his girl. And for another thing, he could usually contain himself. He didn't need to kiss a woman in his car. He usually waited until he could get a woman alone—his private room at the club, her place, the nearest room with a lockable door. He enjoyed women whenever and wherever, but he never did it in public. He dropped a kiss on the end of her nose. "Okay. Let's go."

When he pulled up outside the center, he remembered his visit here with TJ. He'd sat in this very spot while TJ had gone inside. He'd started out worried that she might be trying to con him somehow. He'd felt pretty stupid as he calmed down, and especially after TJ came back out. The center didn't have an online presence because it was as old-school as it got. They didn't have all the permits and licenses they needed, so they flew under the radar to avoid getting shut down. He wondered if Grace would admit that to him. If he was going to get involved in some way, everything would have to be above board.

She let herself out and came around to meet him. He climbed out and met her gaze. He had the feeling he was about to get to know her a whole lot better. He just hoped he'd like what he learned.

She smiled. She didn't seem as if she was trying to work him for help or for a donation. He knew how that felt. People did it all the time. Her smile was so fresh and eager. She wasn't trying to work him; she wanted to share with him. He could tell, even if she wasn't aware of it herself.

"Okay, are you ready for this?"

"I am."

"Saturday afternoon tends to be one of the busiest times of the week. There probably won't be too many kids around, but the vets will be here. There'll be people coming in to the food pantry." She shrugged. "I don't know who will be here. We should just go in and see."

He smiled. "Yeah. Let's go."

He let her go in ahead of him and stopped inside the door to let his eyes adjust. It was so bright out on the street and much less so in here. It was a huge open space. There was an area that looked like a cafeteria with tables and chairs set out at the far end. One corner housed several old worn out sofas and a TV. There was a pool table over in the back.

He thought there was a guy bent down working on the pool table, but when he came into view, he was in a wheelchair. He was an older guy with wild gray hair and steely blue eyes that held an intelligence Oscar hadn't expected to find here. He wheeled himself over to them and smiled when he reached them. The smile didn't have many teeth in it, but the eyes had a lot of questions in them. "You okay, Gracie?"

"Hey, Terry. I'm fine, thanks. How about you?"

He nodded. "Good." He turned to meet Oscar's gaze. "So, you're the moneybags kid?"

Oscar chuckled and held his hand out. "I'm Oscar Davenport. It's nice to meet you, Terry."

Terry shook with him. "How'd you get to be so rich? Did your mommy and daddy give it to you?"

Oscar grinned. He was used to people who expected him to be a trust fund kid, an air-head who hadn't earned his money. "I won't lie. I was born with a silver spoon in my mouth, but my parents took it away when I was eighteen."

Terry frowned at him, and Grace gave him a curious look.

He nodded. "I come from a wealthy family, but my parents are smart people. They made us earn our own way in the world. When I graduated high school, they told me I was on my own financially. I worked my way through college and graduated with no debt. I built a tech company and sold it, then I repeated that a couple of times. Then I learned about investment banking and tried my hand at that. It turned out I was pretty good at it, but it was no fun."

Grace was staring at him wide-eyed. She'd no doubt believed—as most people did—that he'd had a major financial head start in life. He didn't normally disabuse people of that belief. It didn't matter to him what they thought. But this Terry guy was astute, and he obviously wanted to know the measure of the man in front of him. And perhaps that was just an excuse for Oscar to spell out for Grace that he hadn't had everything handed to him in life.

Terry surprised the hell out of him by winking. Oscar got the feeling that he knew all too well that the explanation had been for Grace's benefit as much as his. "Your parents are good people, then. Are you?"

"I like to think so." Oscar looked around. "I'd like to think that I've found my way in life and that I do my bit to help people find theirs."

"And you think building a nightclub is the way to go?"

Oscar met his gaze again. "It's one way to go."

Terry nodded. "What do you think you can do to help here?"

Oscar looked around again. The place was old. It was clean and well-maintained, within its limits. He had a feeling that if an inspector came through, the place would be shut down in a heartbeat. "That's what I'm here to figure out. What does this place mean to you, and what would you do if it closed?"

~ ~ ~

Grace stared at him. He'd said if it closed. Did that mean he was reconsidering?

Terry shrugged. "I'm not going to throw myself on your mercy if that's what you're thinking. We might not have much, but we have some pride left, and we have balls." He smiled at Grace. "Especially her. This place has transformed my life. It's given me shelter; it's given me food." He patted his wheelchair and shot Grace a smile. "It's given me mobility. But more than any of that, it's given me community. If it shuts down, I'll go back under the bridge. That doesn't worry me. I'm an old fart. I've got no future worth crying over. What worries me is that I've gotten to know all these kids." He looked around the center. "The little kids, the kids still in school, the moms with babies who are still kids themselves. The kids who've come back from another stupid war only to be forgotten like we were back in the day. They've all got futures, and if this place goes, those futures don't look too bright. I didn't think there'd be any point telling you all of this. I thought you were just an asshole who wanted to build a club and make more money. Now I've met you, I want to tell you. You can make a difference. You're proud of yourself for what you've done with your life, and I ain't knocking that. All I'm saying is, imagine how proud you'd be if you could do that for all of their lives." He gave Oscar a long, hard stare. "Imagine how proud your parents would be of you then."

Grace held her breath. She'd been determined not to make any impassioned speeches. Oscar was a businessman. She hadn't been convinced appealing to him in that way would work. If she was totally honest, she hadn't wanted to make it personal—hadn't wanted to manipulate the bond she couldn't deny was starting to form between them. Terry hadn't made an appeal. He'd just laid it out the way he saw it, and she imagined it would be hard for anyone not to be touched by that. She turned to look at Oscar and was shocked by what she saw. His face was stony. If he was touched, he was hiding it well. She didn't know what to say. Terry nodded at them and turned and wheeled himself away. She waited, wondering what Oscar would say.

His lips were pressed together into a thin line. This was a new Oscar. She hadn't seen him like this before, and she wasn't sure she liked it. There was a little pulse jumping rapidly in his temple. If she had to describe the way he looked, she'd say he was angry. Shit! Was he? And why? He still hadn't said anything when she saw the front door open, and Spider came striding in. He came straight toward them.

Oscar turned to look at him.

"How are we doing? What do you still need to know?"

Oscar shook his head. "I've seen all I need to see." With that, he turned on his heel and strode out.

Grace's mouth fell open as she watched him go. She'd played out a hundred scenarios of how this visit might turn out. She'd envisioned what she thought was every possible outcome from the disappointing to the beyond amazing. But she hadn't ever imagined this.

Spider gave her a puzzled look. "What's his problem?"

She shook her head. "I'll be damned if I know."

Chapter Twelve

Oscar knocked back his bourbon and then returned to pacing the den. He was angry; angry at himself. Listening to what Terry had to say had been the biggest wake-up call of his life. He was so proud of himself—of everything he'd achieved, and yet listening to Terry, he'd felt ashamed of himself. He shook his head. He shouldn't feel ashamed. He'd done well, and he'd helped people along the way. He did more than most. He stopped in front of the windows and took in the view of the city sprawling out before him. He'd built a great life. It had all come easily to him. Not that he'd been handed anything, but he was a problem solver, an opportunity seeker. He'd done so much that it had all become boring to him. He was opening a second club because he felt as though he'd conquered every challenge, and he couldn't find a new one that excited him.

Terry had made him see that all the challenges he'd sought and overcome were so small and frivolous. How could he enjoy everything he'd achieved when all those people at the center were struggling just to survive? He turned at the sound of a buzzer announcing a car at the front gate. That'd be TJ. He'd called his brother when he got back here. He needed to talk to him.

Ever since TJ had come home, Oscar had tried to ease his way. He'd known his brother was struggling with some demons, but he hadn't really considered what they were. All Oscar had wanted was for TJ to find his way again, to find his way back into the world in which they lived. He'd wanted TJ to enjoy partying again, to find a business venture he could enjoy and make a success. He'd believed that success and happiness could be measured in that way. His chat with Terry this afternoon had made him question everything he'd believed.

TJ appeared in the doorway. "What's up? You sounded weird when you called. I thought you were going to spend the afternoon with Grace."

Shit! Grace! He'd walked out of there. Walked out on her. He stared at his brother.

"Are you okay?" TJ looked at the bourbon on the bar. "Are you drinking?"

Oscar shook his head. "No. Yes. I just had one. I need to call her."

TJ looked worried. "Did you have a fight?"

Oscar shook his head as he dug his phone out of his pocket. He dialed her number and waited. It went to voicemail. "Grace. Please call me. I'm sorry. I need to explain." He hung up and met his brother's gaze.

"Are you going to tell me what's going on?"

Oscar nodded slowly and poured himself another bourbon. "Yeah."

"Do me a favor and slow down with that stuff?"

Oscar knocked it back and then nodded. "Okay." He set the glass down. "What do you think of me?"

TJ frowned. "What do you mean?"

"I mean, do you think I'm an asshole? Am I blind, selfish, stupid?"

"Where's this coming from? Are you sure you didn't have a fight with her?"

"No!" Oscar shook his head in frustration. "It's not about Grace. It's about who I am. What I'm doing. I went into that center with her today, the big shot, the guy with the money who could swoop in and save the day. I left there feeling stupid. Those people are the ones who really live life. They struggle and they get by and they support each other. I've got everything, and I'm feeling good about myself because I can spare a little to help. Grace has nothing, and yet she gives everything." He wasn't sure he was making any sense, but he needed TJ to understand. He had a nasty feeling TJ already did. "I guess my point is, I don't believe in anything. I've never looked for anything outside of myself and the success I can create with money. You're not like that. You believed in something enough to go fight for it. Those people at the center believe in something. They believe in each other, and they believe in helping each other. Grace believes she can change the world or at least the world of the people who need the center."

He sat down and reached for the bottle again, but TJ got it first and moved it away. "You don't need that. You can face yourself without it."

Oscar looked up at him. "You couldn't."

TJ sat down beside him. "I wasn't afraid of facing myself. I used booze, so I didn't have to face everything that happened, over and over and over again." He stared out the window a moment and then turned back to Oscar. "Believing in something outside of yourself isn't necessarily a better way to go, you know. It can literally and figuratively all blow up in your face."

Oscar nodded, wondering how little he really knew about his brother and everything he'd lived through.

"I don't think I have any words of wisdom for you. You're not an asshole. You might have been blind, but there's no law that says you have to dedicate your life to helping a greater cause. You can be happy just doing you."

"I was, but I don't think I can be anymore. I feel like I had one of those road to Damascus moments, and I have to change."

TJ nodded. "If that's how you feel, then that's what you should do. You see what you can do, so do it, but don't do it to make yourself feel better. Do it because you want to and be honest about that. If you do, you'll be on the right track. Don't ever believe that helping other people is somehow better. It's still selfish. It's about what you want to do. That's all."

Oscar nodded. "I didn't mean it like that. I don't mean I think I'm going to be all righteous and good. I mean I'm an idiot for looking for something I can do, and not seeing the obvious. You know the second club was just going to be a stopgap. I was going to throw all of myself into something I don't even care about. Something I do care about is right under my nose. It's not about becoming a do-gooder; it's about finding something I can care about. I'm not saying I want to give a bunch of money and feel better about myself. I'm saying I can share what I've learned. Money's just a tool, a measure of success. If I was a builder, I'd want to help renovate the building, but I'd also want to teach the kids how to use the tools, how to build, share my skills with them in a practical way and pass them on."

TJ nodded. "So, you're not saying you want to throw a bunch of money at the center and leave it at that?"

"No. I'm saying I want to throw a bunch of money in and get involved. I want to help, really help. Not just be on the board but teach the kids about money and how to make it." He shrugged. "Help the vets get back on their feet. See if there's a way all those single moms can do something. I don't know, maybe start a daycare or something for working moms."

TJ smiled. "And the old folk? You're not going to leave them out?"

"No! There must be something I can share with them, show them a way to take their life back into their own hands and ..." He stopped, finally realizing that TJ was teasing him. "Okay, maybe I'm getting a bit carried away, but you get the idea?"

"I do. I get it, and I like it. When I came in, you asked if I thought you were blind or an asshole. I've never thought that. I've always respected that you live life the way you see fit, but I will tell you it's always bothered me that you couldn't see beyond success. Mostly, I managed to convince myself that I was nuts. I was the one who had to go off and fight because of ideals—and look how that turned out. You always seemed to have it all figured out. You seemed happy. Since I've been back, I've noticed that you're not, at least not as happy as I thought. You've been looking for something more. Now you've found it."

"What is it that you think I've found?"

"Meaning."

~ ~ ~

Grace perched on the wall outside the back door of the center. She was still reeling. She couldn't believe Oscar had just walked out like that. She'd gone through everything Terry had said; she'd run it over and over in her mind. She didn't think he'd said anything terrible—anything that should make Oscar leave. She'd thought it inspiring. She sighed and kicked her feet against the wall. What did she know? She and Oscar were very different people, from very different worlds. Maybe he'd taken Terry's words as criticism? That he could and should be doing more with his life. She just didn't know. What she did know was that that he'd left, and their chances of keeping the center going had disappeared with him.

No. She wouldn't allow that to happen. She'd been determined to keep the place going, even if it didn't have a permanent home anymore. She'd been scouting locations and seeking support before she even knew about Oscar Davenport. She could get back to it now. She wasn't going to let him make her give up. She'd been crazy to think that she could get close to a guy like that. The bond—the intimacy she'd thought they shared—was just some sort of illusion.

The door opened, and she tried to smile at Spider as he came out to join her. "I don't know what to say, Gracie."

"Me neither. Except that I feel like a fool."

"Don't. It doesn't sit right with me. He doesn't strike me as the kind of guy who'd just up and walk out."

"He didn't strike me that way either, but that's what he did."

Spider shook his head. "Terry feels like shit. He thinks he chased him off."

Grace jumped down from the wall. "Where is he?"

"In the back, but he doesn't want to talk about it. He thought he was helping. He said he liked the guy so he spoke his mind."

Grace let herself back inside. Terry might not want to talk to her, but she was going to talk to him. No way would she let him go blaming himself. She found him in the little office in the back. He was staring down at his gnarled hands.

"Terry."

He shook his head. "Don't try to talk me up. I blew it for everyone, and I'll live with that. I don't want coddling."

Grace crouched down, so she could look him in the eye. "You know me better than that. I don't coddle. I'm here to tell you to snap out of it. You're smarter than this. Don't let that arrogant prick get to you. The things you said? Any man worth his salt would be thanking you and doing his best to live up to it. If he ran off like that because of what you said, then he's a spineless, worthless piece of shit, and you did us a favor. We don't need that kind around here."

He finally met her gaze and gave her a half smile.

"I'm serious. Now, are you going to sit here feeling sorry for yourself or are you going to make yourself useful? The guy we thought was our best hope of saving this place just walked out on us. We need to get down to work and figure out what Plan B is."

Terry blew out a big sigh. "How can I be useful, Gracie? I'm used up and wore out. I thought I was being useful when I talked to that Oscar."

"I thought you were, too. It's not our fault that he's not the man we thought he was."

He gave her a sad smile. "I had high hopes for the two of you."

"You really are a crazy old coot, then, aren't you?" She smiled, but Terry didn't. Those steely blue eyes of his told her he knew the truth. She was more hurt and upset by this whole thing than he was. "C'mon. We've both lived through worse disappointments than this. Let's go get Spider and the others and see what ideas we can come up with. We're only going to have this place for a couple more weeks. We need to figure out what kind of fund-raising we can do. We're going to need a big pot to rent space somewhere."

~ ~ ~

Oscar picked up his phone. He wanted to try Grace again. What must she be thinking? And why hadn't she called him back?

"Why don't you go over and see her?"

"You think?"

"Yeah, I think. You need to let her know why you walked out of there like that."

"Okay. Let's go."

"To the center or to her place?"

Oscar shrugged. Would she still be at the center? He closed his eyes briefly. She must be thinking that he'd walked out on her—on the center. How stupid was he? "Let's go to the center. Whether she's there or not, I want to talk to Terry. I want to thank him."

TJ smiled. "Isn't he awesome? He's the guy I talked to when I went in there. You know, I was waiting to see what you wanted to do, but now that it looks like you're all in. I want to tell you my ideas."

"What ideas?"

"About what I can do over there."

"I want to hear all about it, but tell me on the way? I need to find her."

In the car, he tried calling her again, but again it went straight to voicemail. "Grace. I need to talk to you. I'm heading for the center, and if you're not there, I'm coming to your place. Call me back if you get this."

TJ looked across at him. "How much of this is for her?"

"What do you mean?"

"You know what I mean."

"No. I don't. Explain."

"Are you suddenly becoming a different person for her?"

Oscar started to protest but stopped himself. He thought about it. Was he? He didn't think so. He'd want to help no matter who'd come to him about the center. If anything, this was for Terry. This was for the guy who'd made him wake up to himself. "No. I want to impress her, of course. I want her to admire me, but up until today, I was fine with her just admiring my financial success—especially since it was useful to her."

TJ nodded. "I think she likes you in spite of your success, not because of it."

Oscar smiled, seeing the truth in that. "You're right. Maybe that's what makes her so special."

TJ smiled.

"What?"

"I'm glad you can admit that she's special. She's different, no two ways about that. She's good for you."

"I hope so. I just need to find her. Right now, she must be thinking I'm a total asshole who walked out on her."

"Yeah."

When they pulled up outside the center again, Oscar sat and stared for a moment.

"Are you okay? Do you want me to go in with you?"

"You don't need to do that."

TJ chuckled. "I'm not offering to hold your hand. I'm hoping it'll only take you a few minutes to set things straight and then you can get started on how you're going to help. I'd like to be in on that. I want to be part of it."

"In that case, let's go." It felt good to have his brother by his side as he opened the door. He felt like he was opening a new chapter of his life, and it was right that TJ was there with him.

He looked around but couldn't see Grace or Spider anywhere. There was a group of older guys sitting watching TV, a couple of kids playing pool, some young women and their toddlers sitting in the dining area, but no one he recognized.

"There he is."

Oscar followed TJ's gaze to where Terry sat in his wheelchair. His eyes held a mix of what looked like sadness and anger. Oscar could understand that. He set out toward him.

"What do you want?" He'd spoken so eloquently earlier. Now he growled and had the look of a sullen old man.

Oscar looked him straight in the eye. "I want to apologize. What you said earlier, you taught me the most important lesson I've ever learned. And instead of thanking you I turned around and walked out. I want to thank you, and I need you to know that I walked out in disgust—at myself. You told it like it is, and I was pissed that I couldn't see it until you said it. I'm sorry."

Those steely blue eyes looked up at him and softened. "You're sorry?"

Oscar nodded. "I am, and I want to thank you from the bottom of my heart."

Terry grinned. "I knew you weren't a worthless piece of shit."

Oscar's heart stopped beating. "Is that what Grace said?"

Terry's grin faded. "Yeah, but she was only trying to make me feel better. I thought I blew it."

"You didn't blow it, Terry. I just hope I haven't. Do you know where she is?"

"Spider took her back to the coffee shop."

"Thanks."

"Are you with him?" Terry asked TJ.

"Yeah. He's my brother."

"That figures. I guess I'll be seeing you both soon enough. You'd best get for now, though. Go find Gracie and make it right."

Chapter Thirteen

Grace sat at the counter and watched Spider work. He had a couple of baristas back there with him, and everything operated smoothly. He had this place figured out. He not only had it under control, but he was growing and expanding the place. Not just the place, but himself. His business was growing, which meant he was able to do more for the center. She, on the other hand, had blown it all. She'd thought Oscar was going to help. She curled her lip—had she really thought he'd be the savior? The knight in shining armor who rode in to save the day. Maybe she had. Maybe she'd gotten carried away. She'd kept telling herself that it wouldn't go anywhere between them, but maybe she'd seen him as her savior, too. As if. She knew better than that, and since she'd apparently needed a little reminder, life had kicked her ass, yet again. Hopes? Dashed. She should know better than to have any.

She'd royally screwed up. She had no way to save the center. In a couple of weeks, she'd be out of a job, but what hurt the most was that she'd managed to misjudge Oscar so badly.

"Chin up, Gracie. We'll figure something out."

"I know, but I think you should take the lead."

Spider made a face. "Yeah, right. You're just feeling sorry for yourself. You're the brains. I'm just backup."

"I'm serious, Spider. You're the one who has it figured out. I was just watching you. You run this place so well. You run your life well. You don't charge into things head first, and you don't spread yourself too thin. You're the slow and steady wins the race guy. I've blown it. You should be the one at the helm."

"You haven't blown anything. You brought Oscar in as a possibility. That possibility didn't pan out. That's all." He shook his head. "I still think you should call him and ask him what happened."

"I don't think so. He could have explained if he wanted to."

"I think he owes you an explanation, and I'm still not convinced it'll be as bad as it looks. I think he's a good guy."

"Ha. I thought that, too."

Spider looked over her shoulder. "Give him a chance."

"He had his chance. He walked out on it." She wasn't about to tell Spider, but he'd also walked out on his chance with her. She was supposed to go to Six with him tonight. They were supposed to spend tomorrow together—she'd thought that was finally going to be their time. But he'd walked out on all of that, on the center, and on her.

"No, I mean, you should give him a chance to explain. Let him talk."

She rolled her eyes. "Even if I wanted to, I couldn't because he walked out and ..."

Spider gave her a warning look. "What I'm saying is he just walked in, and you should."

Grace almost fell off her stool she spun around so fast. There he was. He stood in the doorway and met her gaze. That was no arrogant prick, and he sure as hell didn't look like a worthless piece of shit either. He looked like he'd been through the wringer. What she didn't understand was why.

"Go on," urged Spider. "Go see what he has to say."

"No. Let him come tell us. He owes this to you as much as to me."

"Maybe some of it."

Grace looked at him.

"He's not just here for the center, Gracie; he's here for you."

Grace swallowed and looked back at Oscar who was now making his way to them. He still moved like a big cat, but now he seemed more wary than stealthy.

"Grace."

"Oscar."

"Did you get my messages?"

She shook her head.

"Did you have your ringer on?" asked Spider.

Oh, shit! She had a bad habit of turning the ringer off and forgetting to turn it back on. Still, this was about what he'd done, not about her. She shrugged and tried to look cool, but she wasn't sure she was pulling it off. Her heart was pounding; she could feel the pull to him. He looked so stressed she wanted to go to him and hold him, hug him like they'd hugged last night. She got a grip. "What did you want?"

"To explain. To tell you I'm sorry for the way I ran out of there."

"You don't need to explain. Your actions spoke for themselves."

A flash of irritation sparked in his eyes. "My actions gave you the wrong idea." He looked at Spider who nodded and started to move away as if this was something personal Oscar had to say to her alone.

"Stay." She didn't mean to bark it out like that, but she didn't see why Spider should make it any easier on him.

Oscar looked at him. "She's right. I owe you this as well. I walked out of there, because I was disgusted with myself. Hearing everything Terry had to say was like hearing everything I've been doing wrong with my life. He gave me a moment of truth. He held up the mirror for me, and I didn't like what I saw." He blew out a sigh. "Even walking out the way I did shows you the kind of person I've been. All I could see was what was important to me, and it didn't even occur to me how it would affect you. I didn't walk out because I didn't want to help. I did it because, in that moment, I was so mad at myself I had to get out of there. I had to be alone and come to terms with who I've been and with everything Terry said." He met Grace's gaze. "I'm sorry."

She didn't speak. She didn't know what to say.

"Wow." Spider broke the silence. "That's some apology, dude. Thank you."

Oscar nodded. "Thank you."

Grace continued to stare at him. She wasn't sure she understood and was even less sure that she wanted to turn it all around again so quickly. He couldn't just snatch everything away like that and then come back a couple of hours later and make it okay. Could he? Apparently, he had done. "I don't understand."

He gave her a rueful smile. "I'm saying I'm sorry. When Terry pointed out to me that I'm a selfish prick, the realization made me act like a selfish prick, but I'm over it now. And I plan to change. I'm here to tell you I'm sorry and to ask what I can do."

Grace cocked her head to one side.

"What Terry said made me realize that all the meaning I've been looking for in life can't be found in what I've been doing. It'll never be found in a nightclub, that's for sure. You've offered me the chance to do something meaningful, and I'm all in if you still want me."

Out of the corner of her eye, she saw Spider move away. Oscar stepped closer and held his hand out to her. She slid down from the stool. "You still want to help?"

He nodded. "I do. And I'd still like to keep our deal. If you want to?"

Their deal? It took her a moment to understand. Their deal had been that she'd go out with him tonight—and spend the day with him tomorrow. Part of her wanted to stay mad at him, but it was only a small part. The rest of her was happy and relieved. She took hold of his hand and looked back at Spider who was smiling.

"I'm all in," Oscar told him. "Let's set up a meeting?"

Spider nodded. "Okay. On Monday. For now, you kids get out of here."

~ ~ ~

They spent the afternoon at Oscar's place. Grace said she understood his reaction, but she was different—warier of him than she'd been before. He understood. He couldn't imagine how he would have felt in her shoes. It'd been a bump in the road, for sure, but they could move past it. He was excited to get to work. He knew turning the center around would be much more enjoyable and rewarding than building a new nightclub would have been. He'd wanted to talk about their plans, but Grace had avoided it so far, saying they'd be better to wait until Monday when they could meet with Spider and Terry and some of the others. She was keeping him at arm's length, and he didn't like it, but he knew it'd take time for her to trust him again.

He looked over at her. They were sitting outside on the terrace, and she was staring out into the distance. "What are you thinking?"

"Honestly? I was thinking about Terry."

"I like him. What's his story?"

"He's a Vietnam vet. He was on the streets for years. He's got himself a little studio apartment now."

"No family?"

"None that I know of. He doesn't talk about anything personal."

Oscar wondered what his life must have been like. He was obviously an intelligent man. What led a person onto the streets? And more importantly ... "How did he get off the streets?"

Grace smiled. "The center. He was sleeping in there in the winter. We got to know him and helped him figure out a plan. Do you know how hard it is to get anything done if you don't have an address?"

Oscar hadn't even thought about that.

Grace nodded. "It's tough, to say the least. I don't think Terry would ever have bothered trying to find a place to live if it weren't for the center. He meant it when he said the most important thing it's given him is community. He realized that once he had an address, he could let the other guys use it, too. It's a first step to getting back into society.

Oscar nodded. He knew so little. He took hold of Grace's hand, wondering how she knew so much. "How did you get involved?"

She smiled. "That place has been a part of my life since I was nine."

He lifted his eyebrows.

"I told you about my parents and how Child Services took us. I became a part of the system. When I was nine, I was placed in the same home as Spider for a little while. It was a bad situation. One of my teachers told me about the center, and Spider and I started going there after school."

"Like a homework club?"

She laughed, but there was no humor in it. "I suppose, but more than homework, it was about having somewhere to go and getting something to eat."

"I thought that was what foster homes were for?"

She laughed that same laugh. "That's how it works in theory, but there are a lot of foster parents who are only in it for the monthly payment. The less of that they spend on the kids, the more they have left for themselves."

"Damn. I guess I'm just naïve. I always picture foster parents as being warm, loving people who help out of the goodness of their hearts."

"Don't get me wrong, there are plenty like that. There are people who genuinely want to help. But the system tends to screw them over, too."

"How?"

"They tend to get the troubled kids. Kids who are already using, who've been in trouble with the law, who have major issues—they get placed with the kind-hearted families who want to help. In reality, they can't help. They're not given the support, and they just get a whole load of trouble imported into their lives. It's a lose-lose situation. The kids who don't cause much trouble, who don't have issues, get placed with the sketchier foster parents. They get neglected at best, abused at worst, and tend to go out on their own as soon as possible."

"How soon is as soon as possible?"

"You age out of the system at eighteen."

"And what happens then?"

"Then, you're on your own. It's tough to figure out how to survive by yourself. I ended up on the streets within a few months."

Oscar was appalled, and his expression must have said so.

Grace shrugged. "Don't look like that. I lasted for a while. A lot of kids hit the street the day they turn eighteen."

"Jesus, Grace. My face wasn't about your ability to stay off the streets. I just can't believe that's the way it works. There's no support? No transition?"

"Not much. In California now, you can stay in foster care until you're twenty-one if someone wants to be responsible for you. But most kids are like me. I hated the system, resented having my life dictated by social workers and so-called responsible adults. I couldn't wait to reach independence—even though I had no clue how to deal with all the responsibility that came with it."

"And this is a widespread problem?"

"Err, yeah. Like huge. Anyway. Can we change the subject?"

"Sure. I'm sorry. I had no idea."

"Why would you? It's not part of your world."

It wasn't. He didn't know the first thing about the system or what happened to the kids who went into it—or came out of it.

Grace squeezed his hand and smiled. "Don't look like that. It's not your fault. It's where I come from, and you asked about it. How about you tell me where you come from? Tell me about your family life growing up."

Oscar pursed his lips. He'd led a very charmed life compared to hers. He wasn't sure he wanted to tell her how good his childhood had been.

"Come on. I know it was great, tell me about it."

"Okay. I grew up in Montana. It was my parents, my brothers, and me. They still have the house we grew up in."

"Wow. I've always wanted to see Montana. It sounds so beautiful."

"It is."

"Did you have lots of friends?"

"Some. Hope grew up with us until her mom died, then her dad took her and moved away. We all homeschooled together, but we used to go over to Bozeman to meet up with other homeschool kids for social stuff." He watched her face, wondering how all of that would sound to her.

She looked as though she was listening to a fairy tale. "Tell me more? Did you have ponies and go skiing and stuff?"

He nodded. He'd always said he knew he was lucky to be born a Davenport, but he knew now that he hadn't appreciated just how lucky he was. "Yeah." He hesitated. He didn't like to tell her just how much he'd had as a kid, not when he knew how rough she'd had it, but she was so eager to hear all about it. Somehow telling her felt like he was sharing it with her. "We all had horses and skied and snowmobiled in the winter."

"Snowmobiles? I bet that was awesome."

"It was. We used to float the river in the summer, and sometimes Dad would take us up to the lake so we could water-ski. It was a great childhood."

Grace sighed a happy sigh, as though she was sad to leave the happy picture he'd painted. "Did you live anywhere near Yellowstone? That's a place on my bucket list."

"It is? I grew up half an hour from the north entrance."

"Oh wow. Have you ever seen the buffalo?"

He smiled. He wasn't going to correct her. Buffalo, bison, what did the name matter? She was so thrilled at the idea. He didn't like to tell her that they were so commonplace in the park that he'd never really thought of them as anything special. "Yeah. I have."

"You're so lucky! One day I'll go see them."

"Yeah." One day she would. He'd make sure of it. One day very soon.

She looked at her watch. "What time do I need to be ready?"

"What for?"

A look of confusion crossed her face. "For tonight. I thought ..."

Of course. The plan had been for her to come to the club with him tonight. It didn't hold any appeal now though. At least, not for him. "You want to go to Six?"

"I thought that was the deal."

"It was, but this isn't just about a deal anymore. Not for me. Do you want to go there?"

She met his gaze. "I want to be with you, and that's what you do on Saturday night."

"Not anymore. That's what I used to do on Saturday night. I'm a changed man, Grace Evans, and it's all thanks to you."

She smiled at him suspiciously. "I'm not expecting an overnight transformation, you know."

"Well, you should. This is what I do. My last transformation was from banker boy in the three-piece suit to the sexy nightclub owner you've seen up to this point."

"If you're going do another transformation, could you at least keep the sexy nightclub owner look?"

"You like it?"

"I do."

"Okay. I'll keep the look, but I don't think you want to go to Six tonight any more than I do."

"Where would you rather go?"

He thought about it, then smiled as it hit him. "Do I still have you for the day tomorrow?"

"That's the deal."

"I told you, the deal's off. Do you want to spend tomorrow with me?"

She nodded.

"Okay. Do you trust me enough to surprise you?"

She looked wary again. "Maybe."

"Would anyone miss you if we left tonight and didn't come back until tomorrow night?"

Her eyes widened. "Where are we going?"

"That's the surprise."

She nodded slowly. "I'd have to let Spider know."

"Great. You can call him on the way."

"To where?"

He winked at her. "Wait and see."

Chapter Fourteen

Grace watched out the car window as he drove. She was trying to figure out where they were going, but she couldn't. Oscar had packed a bag and thrown it into his Range Rover, which he was driving himself.

"Are we going to stop by my place?"

He shook his head.

"I need clothes. You got yours."

His hand came up to cover his mouth, but she could still see his smile behind his thumb. "I know, but I figured we could get you some on the way."

She frowned. "Where from? And why? I have plenty of clothes."

"I asked you to trust me. Do you think you can?"

"I suppose." She wasn't sure she liked how this was going.

When he parked the car, she knew she didn't like where this was going. She looked through the windshield at a row of very expensive looking stores. "I don't shop at places like this."

He got out and came around to open her door. "I do. You're going to like it." He took her arm and led her into one of the stores. The name Hayes was written above the door in ornate letters.

Grace looked around. It was way out of her price range, but at least it wasn't one of those snooty stores that made you feel out of place. The atmosphere was warm and friendly. And there was no denying the guy who came hurrying toward them with a beaming smile on his face was warm and friendly. Though Grace had the feeling that all his warmth was directed at Oscar.

"Oscar Davenport, you old devil. How are you?"

Oscar grinned and gave the guy a hug. "I'm great thanks, Roberto. How are you? How's John?"

"We're wonderful, darling, thanks for asking. We had a great night at your place last Thursday."

"Glad to hear it. You two have given Thursday nights a whole new meaning."

He turned to Grace. "Roberto and his partner John are the salsa kings, and they convinced me to make Thursday night salsa night."

Grace smiled at the guy, and he held out his hand. "I'm sorry. I was just so excited to see him. I'm Roberto."

"I'm Grace," she said as she shook with him.

"Is Holly around?" asked Oscar.

"No, she's up at the lake, but she'll be sorry she missed you."

"Give her my best when you see her."

"Will do, and what can I do for you?"

Grace shifted uncomfortably as Roberto eyed her. She was very aware that she was wearing ten-dollar jeans and a thrift store sweater—and he no doubt was, too.

Oscar slid his arm around her shoulders. "We're going on a little trip, and Grace is going to need a few things."

"Ooh!" Roberto grinned and rubbed his hands together. "Where are you going and what do you need, sweetie?"

Grace shrugged. "I don't know; he won't tell me."

Roberto chuckled. "Oh, that's even better." He turned to Oscar. "Do I just have to guess?"

Oscar nodded.

"Great." Roberto winked at her. "Don't worry, darling. I'll do you proud. I'll just need to measure you up."

Grace wanted to feel more uncomfortable than she did while Roberto took every measurement she could imagine—and a few she would never have thought of! When he was done, he sent her to check out the purses while he went and consulted with Oscar.

She picked up a dark brown purse with a light brown pattern on it; it was pretty. Maybe she could get it. She didn't want Oscar to buy her everything. It felt weird. She flipped the price tag and let out a long, low whistle. Nope. No way could she get it—and no way would she, even if she had that kind of money. She could never carry a purse that could have fed a family for a couple of weeks.

Oscar came to join her. "Do you like it?"

She shook her head rapidly and held up her own. "I prefer mine."

He gave her a knowing smile. "Please don't get mad at me about this. I'm only being practical. It's about being able to surprise you. That's all."

She narrowed her eyes at him. "We both know it's not, and part of me wants to be mad at you, but another part thinks it's sweet and knows you mean well."

He rested his hands on her shoulders and planted a kiss on the tip of her nose. She was starting to love the way he did that. "Thank you."

Half an hour later, Roberto returned. Grace eyed all the bags he was carrying then looked up at him.

He grinned. "I've given you a couple of choices."

"A couple? There must be more clothes in those bags than there are in my entire closet."

He gave her a warm smile. "I hope you'll love them all. Let me know, won't you?" He handed her his card, then passed Oscar a receipt.

Grace turned the card over in her hands. Roberto gave her the impression that he genuinely wanted to know how she liked the things he'd chosen for her. She smiled at him. "Thank you."

Oscar hugged him again, and they made their way out.

"Have a lovely time," called Roberto as they reached the door. Grace turned back and waved at him.

She was quiet when they got back in the car.

"Are you okay?" asked Oscar. "You're not mad at me, are you?"

"No. That was a sweet thing to do. Thank you."

"So, what are you mulling over?"

She shrugged. "I'm kind of mad at myself."

"Why?"

"Because he made me realize how small minded I am about some things."

Oscar didn't look too impressed.

"Not because he's gay!" she said quickly. "I don't have a problem with that, and I never understand why anyone does. I mean, if you'd have described that store to me and described Roberto, I wouldn't have wanted to go there. I would have felt, I don't know, superior in some ways and inferior in others. I would have said that's not my kind of place, and he's not my kind of person. I don't value fashion or people who build their lives around it."

"And you think that makes you small minded?"

"In a way. It's not that I suddenly care about fashion. But I do like Roberto. He's not a bad person just because he has different priorities from me. He struck me as a kind, decent human being."

"He is."

Grace nodded. "I guess we both have a lot to learn, don't we?"

Oscar smiled and reached across for her hand. "We do, and I'm looking forward to us teaching each other."

Grace kept her eyes fixed on the road ahead. Did that mean he was looking forward to spending more time with her? She hoped so, but maybe he just meant while they worked on the center.

"Do you want to talk about what you have in mind for the center?" she asked.

"I thought we agreed we should wait? I want this to be about us."

"Us? There's an us?" She regretted the question as soon as she'd asked it. She wanted to know. She wanted the answer to be yes, but she didn't mean to put him on the spot like that.

He reached across and took ahold of her hand. "I'd like there to be. If you're interested?"

She tried to hide her smile, but she couldn't manage it. "I'm interested."

He squeezed her hand, then let it go as he took the exit. "Good."

They were going to Santa Monica. That was good. She liked it there. Maybe they'd walk the beach and visit the pier. It was fancy out here, but it was special. One of the families she'd stayed with had brought her and their other kids out here for their birthdays. It was one of the very few places where she had happy memories. She'd love to make some more here with Oscar.

~ ~ ~

"Have you figured it out?" he asked as he took a right turn.

"I think so."

He grinned. She hadn't. She probably thought they were going to the pier, and one day he'd take her. But that wasn't his plan tonight. Tonight, he was going to take her home. The look on her face when he'd talked about her childhood had touched him deeply. She'd never known anything like that kind of life, and no doubt thought she never would. He wanted to share it with her. His parents still lived in the house he'd grown up in. At least for part of the year. He knew they were there this weekend, and he wanted her to meet them, to feel the kind of love that came with a family like his.

She was looking puzzled now. "This isn't the way to the pier."

"I know."

He'd called ahead to the airport while she was busy with Roberto getting measured up for the jeans and sweaters and cowboy boots he'd wanted her to have. His jet would be ready when they arrived.

"So where are we going?"

"Here," he answered as he turned into Santa Monica Regional.

"It's an airport?"

He nodded and found a spot to park. "Ten out of ten for observation."

She made a face and pushed at his arm. "We're going somewhere else?"

He nodded, trying to hide his grin but not succeeding.

"Where?"

"To check somewhere off your bucket list."

Her eyebrows knit together. "Montana?"

"Yep. Paradise Valley, where I grew up, and tomorrow we'll go down to the park, and you can meet the bison."

"What?" She looked stunned. "But there are no flights to Montana from here." She looked around. "There are no flights to anywhere from here. This place is private."

He cocked his head to one side, trying not to look too smug.

"You have a private plane?" she asked incredulously.

"I do, and we should go get on it. It'll take us about two and half hours in the air."

She sat there staring at him, apparently lost for words, so he got out and went around to open her door for her.

She stood beside him as he pulled his holdall and all of her Hayes' bags from the trunk.

"Are you okay?"

"I'm in shock."

He smiled and slid his arm around her shoulders. "You'll get used to it. Come on. I said we'd be here and ready to go by four-thirty." He steered her inside and felt her tense when the two girls at the front desk spotted them.

"Mr. Davenport!" The blonde whose name he could never remember smiled and batted her eyelashes at him. She usually did that, but Oscar was surprised that she'd do it while he had his arm around Grace. He was grateful, though, as Grace edged closer to him and tightened her arm around his waist.

"Hi—" was all he got chance to say before the other one chimed in.

"I'll let Woody know you're here."

"Thanks." He steered Grace to the sofas that overlooked the runway and set the bags down.

"I can't believe this."

"Believe it. You told me that the place where I grew up is on your bucket list. Why wouldn't I take the opportunity to make it happen for you?"

"Why would you?"

He smiled and rested his hands on her shoulders. "Because I love to see you smile."

It was true, and she rewarded him with one of those smiles. "Thank you."

"Good afternoon, Mr. Davenport. Are we ready?"

"Yes, thanks." Oscar stood back as Woody collected the bags. "And sorry for the short notice."

"No problem." Woody smiled at him. "You're doing me a favor."

Oscar chuckled. He knew the pilot had a somewhat complicated love life and often appreciated the opportunity to get out of town for a few days.

"Do you have a return day in mind?"

"Tomorrow night."

"Okay."

Oscar didn't miss the look of disappointment on Woody's face. He'd love to be gone longer himself, but he and Grace had a lot to get back for. Monday would mark the beginning of his new chapter. His mind was reeling with everything he'd need to do to call a halt to the new club and make a start on the new center. He kept pushing it away, though. That could wait until Monday. His time with Grace couldn't.

They followed Woody across the tarmac to where the jet stood. Grace looked up at him in amazement. "This is yours?"

He nodded.

"Wow!" was all she had to say about that.

~ ~ ~

When they landed at the airport in Bozeman, Grace leaned forward to peer through the window. They'd been flying over mountains for a while now. They were amazing! It was hard to take it all in—the size of the mountains, the sheer vastness. Not to mention the fact that she was sitting in a private jet with the sexiest man she'd ever known. The man who wanted to share this with her.

"What do you think?" he asked.

"I think I'm going to wake up any minute now and realize that this was all just a dream."

He shook his head. "Nope. It's real. It's all real, and it's only going to get better now we're here."

Less than fifteen minutes after stepping off the plane, they were in a rented Jeep and heading east away from the airport. Grace drank in the scenery while Oscar talked on his phone. Apparently, he had a house they were going to. Not only that, but he had someone he could call to open it up for them—and to have dinner delivered. She shook her head as she listened. This was a whole different world.

He hung up and smiled at her. "Everything should be ready when we get there."

"I didn't know you had a house here."

He shrugged. "We all do. It's a great place to visit, and we all want to see the folks, but not necessarily have to stay with them."

She nodded. "Do you come here often?"

"No. I haven't in a long time. We all tend to meet up in LA, or we'll go to Oregon if Dad's busy there."

Grace raised an eyebrow.

"Dad's a doctor," he explained. "He has a rehab clinic on the Oregon coast."

Grace pursed her lips. She knew there was big money in rehab. Celebrities would no doubt appreciate being able to hide out in some secluded, luxury facility with an ocean view. "What kind of rehab?"

"Stroke. He's done some pioneering work in the field. He was a neurosurgeon for most of his career, but when he was ready to slow down, he set up a physical and occupational therapy clinic. Then, when one of his old college buddies had a stroke, he got into that kind of rehab, too. He's the kind of man who always has to be doing something, learning something new."

Grace smiled. "And you take after him?"

"I'd like to think so."

He drove them over a mountain pass, and on the other side, the landscape opened up a little. The wind roared over vast empty plains. Grace was a little sad to leave the mountains behind, but Oscar took the next exit and headed south through a little town that looked to be a gas station and grocery store and not much else. South of town, they squeezed between the feet of two mountains, and then a beautiful valley opened out before them, lined on either side with majestic mountains. Grace leaned her head back and tried to drink it all in.

"Welcome to Paradise," said Oscar with a smile.

After a while, he turned off the main road and down a private driveway.

"Is this it?" asked Grace when she spotted the house.

"That's my parents' place. Mine's just a little farther down the lane."

"Are they there?" she asked when she saw the lights glowing in the windows.

"They are, but we'll see them tomorrow."

Grace shuddered. She hadn't envisioned this as a meet-the-parents type deal.

He reached over for her hand. "Don't worry, they're great people. I think you'll like them."

"I'm more worried about what they'll think of me! They'll probably be horrified that you'd bring someone like me here."

He scowled at her. "What exactly do you mean when you say someone like you?"

She shrugged and stared out the window as they followed the lane and another house appeared. It was beautiful, more like a lodge than a cabin, standing in a meadow by a river, with amazing views of the mountains.

He brought the Jeep to a stop and came around to open her door, but she jumped out before he could. She was perfectly capable of opening her own door.

"Are you going to answer me?"

"You know what I mean. They'll expect you to bring home some model or movie star, someone from a good family at least. Not someone from foster care, someone who's soon to be homeless and jobless again."

He took hold of her shoulders and turned her to face him. "They're not the kind of people who judge someone by their circumstances. Even though it seems you are."

Wow! That told her, didn't it? She glared up at him, but his smile disarmed her, yet again. She couldn't tear her eyes away from his lips, the way they quirked upward did funny things to her insides. The way he lowered them to hers made her forget everything. He crushed her to his chest and claimed her mouth. She clung to him as she kissed him back, hoping this really wasn't a dream she was about to wake up from. She wanted to stay lost in this dream forever, his arms around her, his mouth exploring hers, the birds singing in the meadow, the water rushing in the river, and the big Montana sky darkening above them.

Chapter Fifteen

Oscar showed Grace to one of the guest rooms and left her to go through the Hayes bags. He smiled as he remembered the way Roberto's eyes had lit up when he'd told him what he wanted. Roberto was a great guy, and he had the best fashion sense. He'd even given Oscar a few tips lately. Navy had been his suggestion, and Oscar was grateful for it. He'd mostly stuck to black and gray before, but he now had a collection of navy suits that he loved.

He hadn't seen what Roberto had picked out for Grace, but he couldn't wait. He knew it'd all be amazing. The brief had been clothes suitable for Montana, to include hiking, possible horseback riding, and a possible meal with his parents. He decided to give them a quick call.

"Oscar. You're here then. We saw you go by."

"Hey, Mom. I can't wait to see you."

"You, too, dear. Will you want to come for lunch?"

He sighed. "I'm not sure. I want to take Grace to the park tomorrow. She's never been. So, I don't want to have to race back up the valley for lunch."

"That's okay. How about I do cold plates. That way you can call me when you're on the way back. It won't matter if it's two o'clock or five."

"Thanks, Mom. You're the best."

"I know. I can't wait to meet her."

Oscar smiled. "You don't know the first thing about her."

"I do. I've been pumping your brother for information."

Of course she had. "And what did he tell you?"

"That she's a very special young lady."

"She is."

"And you've known her for how long now?"

Oscar thought about it. Damn. It was less than two weeks.

His mom chuckled down the line. "I already know that too; I just wondered if you'd make any excuses."

He shook his head.

"I'm glad you didn't. Sometimes you meet a person and you just know."

"Know what?"

"That they're your person."

"Your person?" he asked with a laugh.

"Yes, your one and only, your love, the one you're meant to spend your life with."

Oscar didn't know what to say. Grace was special, yes. But to think that she might be his person? That thought hadn't even occurred to him. He was enjoying this for what it was. He hadn't gone so far as to think about what it might be. "I don't know what to tell you, Mom."

He could hear the smile in her voice. "That's okay, dear. I have a feeling, and tomorrow I'll know if I'm right."

He laughed. "You and your feelings."

"Don't mock. You know my feelings are usually spot on."

"I do. I'll see you tomorrow. Say hi to Dad for me?"

"Will do. Bye."

Oscar hung up and went to look out at the view. The huge wall of windows overlooked the river and the valley. He'd chosen this spot because of that view. He let himself out onto the deck. It was almost dark now. The mountains loomed to either side and stars were starting to come out. Could Grace be his person? He sucked in a deep breath. He didn't know. He wasn't ready to have a person. Was he the kind of guy who had a person? A woman. A wife? Damn, that was a scary thought. He didn't understand why people did it—got married. Monogamy was unnatural as far as he was concerned. Why tie yourself to one woman, when there were so many women in the world? Why commit to a lifetime with one person, when people changed, they outgrew each other, they stopped having fun together. He shuddered. No. Grace was a special lady. But he didn't believe he had a person, as his mom put it.

He turned when he heard her at the top of the stairs and went back inside. She leaned against the log railing and smiled down at him. His heart started to pound. Damn, she was beautiful. Her long, dark hair fell around her shoulders. She was wearing jeans and a red shirt. She looked amazing.

"What do you think?"

He grinned. "I can't tell from this distance. You should come down here and let me get a better look." As he watched her make her way down the stairs, his mom's words echoed in his head. Sometimes you meet a person and you just know. He knew a lot of things. He knew she was beautiful. He knew there was some kind of magnetic pull that drew him toward her. He knew his cock sprang to life every time she was close—hell, every time he thought about her.

She reached the bottom of the stairs and stopped. "Well?"

He ran his gaze over her, letting it linger on her rounded hips and full breasts. "I think you're beautiful."

She smiled. "Thank you."

He went to her and circled his arms around her waist.

She smiled up at him. "In case I haven't already told you, I think you're beautiful, too."

"Why thank you." He closed his hands around her ass and pressed his erection against her. "Something's come up that I may need your help with."

She laughed, and to his surprise she reached between them and cupped his cock in her hand. "You mean this something?"

He closed his eyes and nodded.

"But I just put these nice new clothes on," she said as she began to stroke him.

"I think they'd look better on the floor," he murmured.

She chuckled and took his hand. She started back toward the stairs, but he resisted and instead led her out onto the deck.

Her eyes widened. "Out here?"

He nodded and swept his arm out over the view of the valley and then up at the stars. "What do you think."

She nodded. "It's perfect."

~ ~ ~

It really was perfect. If this wasn't a dream, then it was like a scene from a movie. This beautiful house in this beautiful place with this man. This gorgeous, hot, kind, sweet man. He really was sweet. The arrogant prick she'd first met was definitely one facet of his character, but there was no denying he was sweet. An arrogant prick didn't have a house right next to his parents and … oh! An arrogant prick wouldn't be looking at her the way he was now. His big brown eyes were like melted chocolate and they were melting her insides as he led her toward a big wicker sofa. He sat down, and she sat beside him, unable to tear her eyes away from his. He brought his hand up to cup her cheek and brushed his lips over hers. The feel of them sent waves of pleasure rushing through her.

"I want you, Grace."

She nodded. She wanted him, too—so badly, that she couldn't make her mouth form the words. Instead, she leaned in to kiss him, sinking her fingers into his hair and pulling his head down to her.

His hands were on her shirt, unfastening the buttons. She mirrored his movements, eager to see his broad chest. She'd pictured it so often. She knew it would be hard and muscled. And it was. She pushed his shirt off his shoulders and breathed in. He was perfect. She shrugged out of her shirt while he got rid of his, neither of them able to tear their gaze away. Her nipples stiffened under the heat of his gaze. She'd be eternally grateful to Roberto for having picked out this sexy underwear for her. The bra was a little snug, but that might not be a bad thing. Judging from the way Oscar was feasting his eyes on her breasts, it was definitely a good thing that her full breasts were straining the cups and spilling over.

He dropped his head and she moaned as he dipped his tongue into her cleavage. Her belly tightened, and shock waves ran from her nipples straight to the place between her legs that was throbbing in hope of the same treatment.

His hands were behind her back, unhooking the bra and allowing her breasts to spill free. Their freedom was short lived as he filled his hands with them and ducked his head, this time lavishing each taut peak in turn with his hot, hard tongue. She squirmed in her seat and the seam of her jeans only intensified the pleasure rippling through her. The pressure felt so good against her, but it wasn't the pressure she wanted.

She unzipped him, and he returned the favor. Then they stood, face to face, the tiny scrap of silk that Roberto had thought would serve as panties, and his navy boxer briefs the only things keeping them apart.

"You're beautiful, Grace."

She nodded. She wasn't interested in words right now. "Fuck me, Oscar."

His eyes widened in surprise. For a moment she thought he might protest, but he didn't. He nodded and pushed his boxers down.

Double damn! She'd known he was big, but to see him in all his glory was something else. She licked her lips. She couldn't help it, and that encouraged that smug little smile of his.

He took hold of himself and stroked the length of his shaft. She watched, mesmerized.

"Do you want some of this?"

She nodded and swallowed—hard. "I want all of it."

He sat down on the sofa and drew her to him. Once she was standing straddling his legs, he filled his hands with her breasts again, and began to work his magic with that tongue. She sank her fingers in his hair and let her head fall back. She shivered as he dropped his head and kissed her ribs working his way slowly down. He parted her thighs with both hands and smiled up at her. She wanted to tell him to hurry and quit fooling around, but she waited, eager to see what moves he had for her.

He gave her pussy the same treatment he'd given her breasts. He held her open with his thumbs and tormented her with his tongue, licking and sucking until she wanted to scream. He closed his mouth around her clit, and she screamed as she started to come. He dug his fingers into her hips and held her away from him. Her scream turned to a moan as her orgasm faded before it got started. He grinned up at her and she scowled. "I was almost there."

"I know." He dipped his hot hard tongue inside her and she was there again, drawing in ragged breaths as he took her closer and closer ... and then stopped.

"Oscar!"

"Yes, Grace?"

"What are you doing to me?"

"I'm getting you ready."

"I am ready! I'm more than ready."

He brought his hand up to cover his smirk, then sucked on his thumb. It was a sight that took her straight back to the edge. He withdrew it from his mouth and circled her clit with it. She moved her hips in time with him, desperate now for the release that was so close.

She closed her eyes in disappointment as the pressure from his thumb ceased, then she screamed again as he thrust it inside her. All her inner muscles tried to tighten around it, but it wasn't enough. She was half sobbing, half gasping when he pulled her down onto his lap. She wrapped her legs around his waist as he guided himself to her entrance. Then he thrust his hips and entered her, filling her, stretching her, and sending her mind spinning away. She was no longer capable of coherent thought. All she could do was gasp in ragged breaths as his hands closed around her ass and he started to move inside her. She was lost. She was coming apart at the seams. The only solid thing in her universe was the thick, hard shaft that was filling her, pounding inside her over and over. Her breasts were bouncing as she rode him. He flicked her nipple with his tongue and then took it inside his mouth, making her scream once more.

It was enough to tip her over the edge. Her belly tightened and her inner muscles followed suit.

"Oscar," she breathed.

"Do you want it?"

"Yes," she gasped.

He was pistoning his hips, pulling her down hard to receive every thrust. "Take it," he gasped. "Take it, take it, take it!" He found his release deep inside her and it triggered her own. She clenched him and drew him deeper and deeper inside with every thrust.

"Look up," he gasped.

She could barely process the words, but when she did, she let her head fall back as he thrust deeper and deeper. It was magical, wave after wave of pleasure crashed though her as she stared up at that big starry sky. As their bodies moved frantically together, she could no longer distinguish the stars in the sky from the ones exploding inside her head.

When they finally stilled, he rested his head against her shoulder and turned to nibble the sensitive skin on her neck.

"Ooh!" She held on tight as an aftershock rippled through her His fingers digging into her ass told her it got to him, too.

"That'll teach you," she said with a chuckle.

"What, to always make sure I nibble your neck?"

She shook her head and slid down from his lap. Why would he say such a stupid word as always?

He looked puzzled. "Something wrong?"

"It just dawned on me that we were a little irresponsible there."

He sighed. "Sorry, it dawned on me about a minute too late. I'm clean."

"Me too."

He nodded, she knew he didn't want to ask the question, but she wasn't going to make it easy for him.

"Are you on the pill?"

He controlled his expression pretty well when she shook her head, but he did turn a shade paler.

She laughed. "I'm not, but I have a coil. You've got no worries there."

He breathed a sigh of relief. "Sorry."

"Don't be. We were both stupid." She shifted uncomfortably. Not using a condom could have some very major downsides, but she'd been fairly confident there wasn't much risk. A guy who screwed around as much as he did, would no doubt get himself checked regularly. However, there were some minor downsides, too, and right now she needed to go clean up. She landed a kiss on his cheek. "If you'll excuse me, I'll be right back," she said as she collected her clothes.

~ ~ ~

Oscar watched her go back inside. He couldn't believe how monumentally stupid that had been. He always used a condom—without fail. Was he crazy? Yes, Grace was special in so many ways, but if he were to take his hormones and his feelings out of the equation, she was the last woman he should be taking any risks with. That would have to be the one and only time he did.

Grace was still upstairs when he emerged from the guest bathroom on the main floor. He was glad of a few minutes to himself. He was getting too swept up in all of this and he needed to slow down. He went to the wine cellar and selected a bottle of his favorite Bordeaux. He didn't even know if she drank wine. He knew she could knock back beer and bourbon ... he shook his head. See. He didn't know the woman, not really. His mom's voice echoed in his mind. Sometimes you meet a person and you just know. Yeah, maybe, but other times you let your dick do all the thinking and you screwed up—big time.

He went to the kitchen and opened the fridge. It was filled with trays from Wild Horse Catering up in town. He turned the oven on to preheat and poured two glasses of wine, wondering what was taking her so long.

A few minutes later, she came back downstairs.

"Everything okay?" he asked.

"Yes, why wouldn't it be?" Her prickly tone surprised him, but he let it go.

"No reason. Are you hungry?"

"I'm starving. What have we got?"

He smiled. That was another way she differed from the women he usually dated. They never ate; they'd never admit to hunger. "We've got a pasta bake and some garlic bread and a big green salad. How does that sound?"

"Sounds great. What do you need me to do?"

He handed her a glass of wine. "Take a seat and drink that."

She took the glass and swirled it. "I'm not much of a wine drinker, but I'll give it a go."

"See what you think. We can find you something else, if you don't like it."

She took a sniff, not like someone trying to impress him by going through the motions of wine tasting—more like someone who was checking to see if the milk was spoiled.

He laughed. "Try it."

She took a teeny sip, then nodded. "Hmm, that's not bad. I could learn to like this stuff."

"Good. It's one of my favorites."

She smiled. "In that case, thank you for sharing it with me."

He nodded but didn't reply as it dawned on him that he didn't usually share it. This particular wine was one he saved for his alone time. So, why had he wanted to share it with her?

Chapter Sixteen

Grace peered at Oscar's parents' house as they passed it on their way out. It was beautiful—not just because it was a beautiful building, but because she could tell it was a lovely home. It was magnificent, but not cold and sterile. It looked loved and lived in. There were flower beds around the front door that someone obviously lavished with care. She doubted they'd get a gardener out here in the middle of nowhere, so one of his parents must do it.

It was strange. Part of her wanted to think of his parents as aloof, rich, and snooty, but everything she saw and heard suggested that they were kind and loving. She made a face. And Oscar thought they weren't so different? They couldn't be more different. He had everything she didn't. Not just money—he had real wealth; he had family. People who loved him. People he loved. He had security and stability and history. She blew out a frustrated little sigh.

"Are you okay?" asked Oscar as he reached the main road and came to a stop before turning out onto it.

"Yeah, I'm great. I can't believe we're going to Yellowstone. I'm making a start on my bucket list."

He pulled out and headed south with a smile. "This is the first item you get to cross off?"

She nodded.

"You'll have to tell me what else is on there. We can work our way down the list."

She pursed her lips. She'd been trying not to think too much about what was going on here—what was happening between them. This little trip was amazing, and tomorrow they'd get to work on what exactly he planned to do for and at the center. But she was trying not to think beyond that. If she allowed herself to think about it, she might wonder if there could be any kind of future between them. She pressed her lips tighter together, because that was totally ridiculous!

He shot her a questioning look, misinterpreting her silence. "Come on, tell me. What else do you want to do before you die?"

She shrugged. "Most of it's just personal stuff, you know, things I want to achieve. Nothing you could help with."

"Nothing you want to tell me about?"

"No." She said it a little more firmly than she'd intended, but it had the desired effect of ending the conversation. As they drove on in silence, she felt bad. He was only trying to be nice to her.

She forced herself to stop thinking about what would be on her bucket list if she thought Oscar was going to feature in her life. There was no point going there. "What about you?" she asked. Hearing what was on his bucket list would no doubt reinforce how unlikely it was he'd ever feature in her life. He'd have ambitions and dreams that wouldn't allow room for someone like her.

He smiled. "I don't have one."

She turned to look at him. "You don't?"

"No. Not a list of things I'd like to do before I die, as such."

"Something else then?"

He nodded. "I tend to have a list of things I want to do and be each and every day."

"Wow. What's on your list for today?"

He smirked. "Today I want to make you happy."

A shiver ran through her. He was most likely the first person who'd ever had that goal. It made her insides warm and fuzzy, until she reminded herself that it was only for today. Nothing more. "Thank you. Is that all?"

He laughed. "Isn't that enough? I think it's plenty, but there are a few other things, too. I want to see my folks. I want to visit the park, for me as well as for you. I haven't been down there in years." He glanced across at her and smirked. "I want to get laid."

She laughed. "And you will. Is that a goal that you set every day?"

He shrugged. "Mostly."

She was mad at herself for asking—she'd already known the answer. She didn't need to rub her own nose in it.

"Does that bother you?"

She shook her head vigorously. "No. Why would it? I was just curious." It really didn't bother her. She knew that was a part of who he was. He was a young, healthy, wealthy, attractive guy. She'd expect him to have that goal. She'd be over the moon about it if his goal was to have sex with her every day.

That seemed to kill the conversation for a while, and Grace sat back, content to drink in the amazing scenery that surrounded them. The valley was long and narrow, and the Yellowstone River ran alongside the road. Mountains loomed over them to the east and the west, but they didn't feel oppressive. They felt more like benevolent guardians watching over them as they passed. It was easily the most beautiful place she'd ever seen, and she wouldn't be surprised if it was the most beautiful place on earth.

~ ~ ~

By lunchtime, Oscar had given Grace a whirlwind tour of the major attractions in the northern half of the park. There was far too much to see to do it all in one day. You could spend weeks here and not see everything you wanted to. He was pleased that she'd gotten to see the bison—wandering around the parking lot at Mammoth and holding them up on several of the roadways. They'd seen elk, too, and a stop to investigate why a dozen cars had pulled off the road had been rewarded with a glimpse of a wolf which had thrilled Grace to no end.

He enjoyed spending time with her. She was unlike the women he usually went out with. For starters, he doubted any of them would have wanted to come here. He knew for a fact he wouldn't have brought any of them to meet his parents. He frowned. Why had he brought Grace? He knew the answer to that. He wanted her to know what it felt like. Maybe that was fucked up? She didn't have a loving family, had never known one. He just wanted her to be able to bask in the warmth of his for a little while. But maybe it was wrong? Maybe it'd be tormenting her with what she didn't have.

They were walking back to the parking lot where they'd left the Jeep while they'd taken a walk around the Grand Prismatic Spring. He'd bought Grace a camera in the gift shop when they arrived, and she'd been snapping away at everything in sight. He stopped when she tugged on his sleeve. "Are you okay?"

"Yeah. Why?"

She shrugged. "You just got this look on your face like you were mad about something."

"No. My mind tends to race through all kinds of things. I don't know what I was thinking, but it wasn't anything important." There was a first. He wasn't telling a woman the truth. Normally he told them whatever he thought; not only was it the right thing to do, but it made life a lot simpler. He didn't string them along. He told them he wouldn't call them; he told them they'd most likely see him with another woman the next time they came into the club. So, why hadn't he admitted to Grace that he'd been mad at himself for doing something that might upset her? Because he cared about her? That was fucked up. Why would he be honest with women he didn't care about and lie to the only one that he did? And since when did he care about her?

They'd started walking again and she was studying his face. "Did I do something wrong?"

He slid his arm around her shoulders and hugged her into his side as they crossed the bridge that spanned the river. "No. You didn't do a thing wrong." He smiled. "Let's take a picture." He took the camera from her hand and backed them both against the railing. This wasn't going to work. He gave it back to her and pulled his phone out instead. After he'd taken a bunch of photos, he took hold of her hand and they headed back to the Jeep. Grace surprised him when she let go and hurried over to an older couple. He smiled when he realized that she was asking them to take a photo for her.

He posed with her and smiled and goofed around as the old guy seemed to be quite the photographer. Oscar planted a kiss on Grace's cheek hoping he'd get a good photo of that.

"Perfect! I hope they turn out." He handed the camera back with a smile.

Back in the car, Oscar sent his picture to Grace's phone. "Can I have the ones from the camera, too?"

She nodded. "Sure."

He couldn't shake the feeling that she wasn't going to send them to him, and that bothered him. He wanted those photos. They were memories of their first trip here.

~ ~ ~

Once they were out of the park and headed back up the valley, Oscar reached across and took hold of Grace's hand. She loved it when he did that.

"Do you want to go to my parents' for lunch?"

She nodded. "I thought that was half the reason we're here—so you can see them."

He made a face. "I asked if you want to go."

Oh. She hadn't thought about that. Maybe he'd rather go by himself—and not be embarrassed by her. "No. That's fine. I can hang out at your place. You go. I bet they're dying to see you."

He scowled and pulled off the road. He looked mad!

"What?"

He shook his head and reached across to cup her face between his hands. "Why do you always count yourself out? I was asking if you wanted to go, if you were okay with it, because I want you to enjoy yourself. Why did you assume that I didn't want you to go?"

She shrugged.

"We're not going anywhere until you explain it to me."

She rolled her eyes. "I don't know what to tell you. I thought you might want them to yourself."

"And what else?"

She dropped her gaze and fiddled with her fingers.

"Tell me."

"Okay. I was surprised that you wanted me to meet them in the first place. I figured maybe you'd had second thoughts and didn't want them to meet me."

He blew out a sigh and planted a kiss on her lips. "Why are you so down on yourself?"

"I'm not. I'm just very aware of how different we are."

"And I've already told you that I don't see the difference, and my parents won't either. If I'm honest, I wanted you to meet them so that I could share them with you, show you what it feels like to have a loving family. Then I wondered if that was wrong, whether it would make you feel bad instead of good."

Grace stared into his eyes for a long moment. He was trying to do something nice for her and was second-guessing himself. She blew out a sigh and rested her forehead against his.

"That's incredibly sweet of you, you know."

His lips quivered up into his now familiar smirk. "But was it a good idea or a mistake?"

"I don't know. I love the idea. I'd like to meet them, even though it's a bit scary. I'd love to feel how it feels to be with a family like yours, but I can't guarantee how I'll feel afterward. Maybe I'll be happy and grateful you shared that with me, and maybe I'll feel sad about everything I never had. I don't know."

"Do you think it's worth the risk of finding out?"

She nodded. "I do. Nothing ventured, nothing gained."

She smiled to herself as she listened to him talk to his mom on the phone. No one had ever tried to do something like this for her before. She'd always wondered what it was like to have a family, but she didn't know where any of her siblings were and didn't care where her mom might be. Growing up, most of her friends were the kids of single moms and parents who worked two and three jobs and were never around.

She sat up straight when he pulled off the main road.

"Don't be nervous." He gave her hand a squeeze.

"I'm not."

"Good. I think you'll like them."

She did. They were both warm and friendly. They made her feel welcome, and she just knew they didn't see her the way she'd expected them to—as somehow less than them. They welcomed her into their home and treated her as though she and Oscar had been friends forever. They told her

embarrassing stories about when he was a kid. It was
wonderful.

After lunch, his dad—Johnny as he'd asked her to call him—
asked if he could borrow Oscar. Grace nodded happily. Before
she'd met them, she might have imagined that such a move
would be his dad pulling him aside to ask why he'd brought
her. Now, she could tell he was eager to catch up with his son
about business or some guy stuff.

His mom smiled at her. "Is it too early for a glass of wine?"

Grace grinned. "Never."

"Do you prefer red or white?"

Grace shrugged. "Whichever's easiest."

His mom raised an eyebrow. "You don't have a preference? I
thought everyone did."

Grace looked over her shoulder as if someone might overhear
her embarrassing secret. She didn't mind telling Jean. "I really
don't know. I don't normally drink wine. I had my first glass
of red last night."

If Jean was shocked, she didn't let it show. Instead she leaned
in with a smile. "Do you want a beer? I have some."

Grace laughed. She couldn't imagine Jean drinking beer. "I'd
love one."

"Come on, then." Jean led her out onto the deck and down
the steps to the yard. When they reached a greenhouse, Jean let
them in with a conspiratorial smile. "I spend a lot of time out
here, and when you get thirsty, a glass of wine is no use.
Nothing hits the spot like an icy, cold beer." She went to an
under-the-counter fridge and pulled out two beers. Grace
couldn't help laughing as she popped the tops off them like a
pro.

"Thank you. I didn't expect you to be a beer drinker."

Jean shrugged happily. "I kind of got that impression. Do I
come across as a snob?"

"Oh, God, no! I didn't mean that. I thought you might be, before I met you, but I know better now. I'm sorry."

Jean put a hand on her arm and smiled kindly. "Don't be. I was only teasing. It seems to me that you thought we were going to judge you harshly and you judged us that way."

Grace felt bad.

"It's okay. I'm just glad you like us now you know us."

"Not as glad as I am that you like me."

Jean clinked her bottle against Grace's. "Here's to the beginning of a beautiful friendship."

Grace didn't know what to say.

"Don't look like that. You and Oscar are just getting started."

"No. He's just being kind to me."

Jean threw back her head and laughed. "Oh, dear. You haven't figured it out yet, either?"

"Figured what out?"

Jean shook her head. "Much as I want to, I'm not going to spell it out for you. I'll let the two of you figure it out for yourselves."

Grace frowned. Jean thought they were just getting started? No. They weren't. She'd like that to be true, but it wasn't realistic. She'd never had a relationship that lasted more than a few months. That wasn't the way her life worked. Jean was watching her, and she felt like she had to say something, to explain. "He's not looking for a relationship, neither am I."

"That's usually when it happens, dear."

Chapter Seventeen

On Monday morning, Oscar stood in his dressing room and looked around. He'd been about to put on his usual white shirt and blue suit, but now he was second-guessing himself. He was going to the center to meet with Spider and Terry. Was a suit the most appropriate, or should he wear jeans and a T-shirt? He gave himself a rueful smile in the mirror. Grace was really getting to him—or at least her more judgmental side was. She'd admitted that she thought of him as an arrogant prick. Maybe he should be trying to give a different impression to the others? He reached for his suit. Fuck it. It was a part of who he was. Just because Grace was doing strange things to his head—and his body—he wasn't going to start changing who he was.

Hell, she wasn't even going to be there until tonight. She had to go to work—for Harry. A job she wouldn't have much longer once the sale of the center went through. He shook his head. He'd managed to inadvertently turn her world on its head. To be fair, she was doing the same to him.

He was starting to believe his mom's theory about everyone having a person—the one person they were meant to be with. More than that, he was starting to believe that Grace was his person. It was crazy, but it felt true. He sighed and finished getting dressed. He wasn't sure that she felt the same way; in fact, if he had to bet on it, he'd say she didn't. She'd been grateful for the trip to Montana, and she was enthusiastic about his upcoming involvement in the Center, but he wasn't convinced that she would ever see him as part of her life—her future. He shuddered. Maybe his mom had just gotten to him? She'd fallen in love with Grace, there were no doubts about that. His dad had, too, but maybe they were just relieved that he'd finally brought a woman to meet them. He introduced them to plenty of women before, but only on social occasions where he'd been with a date. He'd never brought anyone home before—never wanted his family to meet a woman or for a woman to meet them

He started at the sound of the front door opening.

"Are you ready?" called TJ.

"Be right out." He checked himself over in the mirror and went out to join his brother who was in the kitchen, pouring himself a cup of coffee.

"What's the plan for the day?"

Oscar blew out a sigh. "Not much, just cancel a new nightclub and set up a new charity instead."

TJ chuckled. "A quiet day then."

"Yeah, nothing out of the ordinary."

"Okay, so where to first?"

"To the office at the club. I have a lot of calls to make."

"Anything I can do?"

Oscar met his brother's gaze. TJ had been a mess when he first came home—spending most of his time drinking and staring at the wall. He'd been doing better since he'd been driving for Oscar, but he'd made it very clear that he'd take things in his own time. Being a chauffeur wasn't his goal in life, but it was enough for the time being—or at least it had been until now.

"Is there anything you'd like to do?"

"I'd like to be involved; I think I can be useful."

Oscar waited.

"I'd like to get involved at the center with the vets and wherever else I can help. I spent some time there over the weekend, just hanging out talking to the guys. We're all in the same boat in some respects, except I'm in a better position than most. I think it's about time I stop feeling sorry for myself and start being useful."

Oscar grinned. "That's awesome."

TJ smiled back. "Thanks for not saying it's about time."

"I didn't say it because I don't think it. You'll get there in your own time or not at all."

"Anyway." It seemed TJ didn't want to get bogged down talking about himself and his own progress. "What needs to happen? I'm guessing you're going to need to go through all kinds of inspections and permitting processes and a whole boatload of red tape. The sooner we can get those balls rolling, the better."

"Absolutely. The first thing I need to do is talk to the lawyers and the accountants. I don't know if this should be set up as a nonprofit or a charitable trust. We've got a hell of a lot of work to do. I don't think they have any permits right now, and that's a whole can of worms I'm not looking forward to."

TJ smiled. "I can deal with all of that. I mean, we're going to have to check out zoning, insurance, safety regs, and a whole bunch more, I'm sure."

"You want to take on that kind of thing?"

"Yeah. I do."

"Great. Then let's get to the office and get to work. I'm going to be busy with legal and financial, and I'm meeting with Spider and Terry at two."

"You mean we are?"

"Yeah. I guess I do."

"And what about Grace?"

"She's at work."

TJ downed the last of his coffee and made a face. "I didn't think about that. She just volunteers her time, outside of her job, right?"

"Yes, although she's not going to have that job for much longer. Once the sale goes through, Harry Dressel plans to retire."

"Why do I get the feeling that she won't have to worry about a job?"

"What do you mean?" Oscar's heart started to pound. Even if Grace was his person, he still wasn't sure about the whole getting married thing—and definitely not this soon. And besides, even if they did get married someday, he couldn't see Grace wanting to be a kept woman. It just wasn't her.

TJ gave him a puzzled look. "From what I understand, she practically runs the center. I assumed we'd make that official and employ her."

"Oh." Oscar felt dumb. "Yeah."

TJ picked the car keys up off the counter and headed to the garage. "Are you going to tell me about your trip up home?"

Oscar didn't reply until they were both in the car and TJ started to pull out of the garage. "No. I don't think I am."

TJ smirked. "I didn't think so, but that's okay. Mom already filled me in."

"She did?"

"Yeah. She agrees with me—Grace is special."

Oscar shook his head. She was. But he didn't know what that would mean.

~ ~ ~

It was six o'clock by the time Grace made it to the center. Work had been crazy busy. Harry was wrapping everything up. She'd assumed it'd take him a while after the sale went through to wrap up all his client accounts and transfer them to other

CPAs. She'd been wrong. He'd gone into overdrive and was nearly ready to close up shop now.

She got off the bus, wondering what she was going to do. Louise had told her time and again that she didn't need to worry about the rent until she found a new job. Spider had told her he'd give her all the shifts she could handle at the coffee shop, but she needed to find something. She didn't want to depend on her friends to carry her through. She stood on her own two feet.

She took a deep breath before she opened the front door. It was time to switch her mind away from her own problems and onto the center. She'd love to think its problems were over, but she was waiting to see. Oscar was stepping in to save the place. She didn't know yet what that would look like, and she wasn't even sure how long it would last. So, she needed to get inside and find out. She did, but she needed a minute to prepare herself. She'd just spent an amazing weekend with the man. He'd taken her to Montana, to Yellowstone, and more than that, he'd taken her to meet his family. That was huge! But, at the same time, it was completely separate and apart from whatever he was doing here at the center. He'd wanted her to stay with him last night when they got back to LA. It was going on midnight and she'd been tempted, but she insisted he drop her at Louise's. Did she want to spend the night with him? Of course she did, but she'd felt the need to break away from him, to draw a clear line between the guy and the girl who'd met in the elevator, and the center manager and her benefactor.

"Are you going to go in, or are you just warming the doorknob?"

She swung around to see Terry sitting behind her. "Hey, you."

"Hey yourself. Is everything okay? They're all waiting for you. We got a lot done this afternoon."

"You did?" For some reason, that bothered her. It shouldn't. The whole point of bringing Oscar on board had been so they could make progress, figure out a future for the place, but now that he was here and apparently doing just that, she felt excluded. Which was ridiculous, and she knew it.

"Yeah, come on in, so we can tell you all about it."

She held the door open and followed him inside. Her breath caught in her throat somewhere when she spotted Oscar. He was sitting on the floor with a bunch of little kids running around him and over him. It was the most unexpected sight. He looked up and met her gaze with a smile that blew her away—it wasn't cocky or arrogant, and it wasn't one of his smoldering looks that made her stomach flip. It was just a genuine, fresh, happy smile. She smiled back.

He got to his feet and plucked a couple of kids off his leg as they tried to cling to him.

Terry chuckled beside her. "You're not the only one who's fallen in love with him, Grace. I think you've got some serious competition for his affection there."

Grace sputtered. "Fallen in love with him?" She glared at Terry. "You're back to acting crazy."

Terry just shrugged. "I'll let you two have a minute while I round everyone up. There's a lot to tell you."

Again, she had that weird feeling. She didn't like being excluded. She got over it quickly when Oscar reached her and put a hand on her shoulder. "Hello, beautiful."

"Hey."

"I missed you today."

Wow. She hadn't expected that.

"When we get done here, will you have dinner with me?"

She nodded. She needed to eat, and she didn't have any other plans. It'd be rude to say no after the weekend he'd given her.

"And stay with me afterward?"

She met his gaze. Still no cockiness, no smirk, just a question in his eyes. She nodded again. She could make a dozen excuses—about work in the morning and needing to get home and not having a change of clothes—but they'd only be excuses. She didn't know what was going on with him, but she didn't need to. She needed to stop complicating it. A hot guy, who she already knew was great in bed, had just asked her to stay the night with him. Why would she say no?

"Hey, Gracie, come on." Spider waved them over to where they'd pulled four of the cafeteria style tables together.

Oscar put his hand in the small of her back as they made their way over. It seemed as though heat radiated out from his fingertips and flowed through her whole body. Hell yeah, she'd stay with him tonight—and it would only be because he made her so horny. It would have nothing at all to do with the fact that being so close to him again made her feel relaxed, and happy—like she'd come home.

~ ~ ~

The week flew by. It was Friday before Oscar had a chance to catch up with himself. They'd made a lot of progress. TJ was taking care of all kinds of red tape—and mending fences with various departments of the city and county governments which Grace had managed to sidestep for the last few years.

Oscar had spent his days in a whirlwind of meetings and phone calls. He'd broken contracts with suppliers he'd had lined up for the new nightclub. He'd managed to switch some of the contractors over to do work for the shelter, but he'd trodden on some toes, too. So, be it. It was all for the greater good.

TJ had come back to life in a big way. He worked tirelessly with the bureaucracy and then spent the rest of his time with the vets. Oscar was glad he'd found a purpose again. He wasn't over his own trauma, not by a long shot, but it was obvious that helping other guys was helping him.

Grace had only been able to join them in the evenings. He knew that bothered her, but he didn't know what to do about it. She still worked for Harry and had said several times that she intended to stay with him until the day he closed his doors for good. Oscar knew he should talk to her about what her plans were after that, but he hadn't made the time yet. They'd stayed at the center until going on ten o'clock every evening. He and Grace, and Terry, Spider, and TJ had naturally formed a kind of leadership committee, but there was a whole bunch of other people who stayed late and worked hard every day too.

He looked around. TJ was playing pool with a bunch of the guys. A gaggle of oldies were chatting in the cafeteria area. Spider and Grace were standing outside the pantry having what looked like a heated debate. Oscar frowned. He'd hate for the two of them to fall out. He'd been skeptical when Grace had first told him that Spider played the big brother role in her life. He'd expected to have trouble with the guy at some point. He didn't know many men who played that role without a vested interest. Spider was one of the few exceptions. The more time he'd spent with them, the more he'd realized that they really did have a brother sister relationship. Although, they didn't normally fight.

He took a few steps toward them.

"… I need the work." Grace was glowering at Spider.

If she'd been looking at Oscar that way, he was pretty sure he would have backed right down. Spider didn't.

"No. What you need is to get a life, and it seems to me, this week you've had one. So, no. I don't want you to come in and work. I want you to go home with him."

Oscar pursed his lips. Grace had come home with him every night this week. He'd assumed that she would tonight, too. They planned to knock off at eight since it was Friday.

"You've got a band tonight. You need the help, and I'm only going to have a job for another week. So, I need the money."

Oscar sighed. Damn. He hadn't known things were that bad for her. He wanted to make it right. It was time to talk to her about her role at the center going forward. They were setting up as a nonprofit so the center could employ her. He just hoped that she wouldn't get too touchy about the fact that he was the only source of funds the nonprofit had—so effectively he would be paying her wages. It wasn't a conversation he was looking forward to. He knew how independent she was, and he also knew that she didn't want to feel beholden to him—in any way.

Spider caught sight of him and rolled his eyes. "Can you talk any sense into her?"

Oscar doubted it. He went to join them. "What's the problem?"

Grace turned her angry stare on him. "I need to work, and my so-called friend here is taking my shifts away."

Spider shook his head and blew out a sigh. "Your so-called friend is trying to do you a favor. You're beat, Gracie. You've been working your ass off for Harry all week, and then coming and working your ass off here, too. I don't want you keeling over from exhaustion while you're working for me."

"I was hoping you were going to have dinner with me," said Oscar.

"I was, but I forgot he has a band playing tonight. He needs the staff, and I need the money."

"I don't know that I can help with waitstaff, but I've been thinking about your situation. I wanted to talk to you about it tonight."

She put her hands on her hips. He knew it was never a good sign when a woman did that, but it still turned him on when Grace did it. Then again, it seemed everything she did turned him on.

"What do you want to talk about?"

Spider grinned at him and began to back away. He'd effectively diverted Grace's anger onto Oscar, and now he was about to beat a sneaky retreat. Awesome!

"Can we get out of here and go grab something to eat? I need beer and meatloaf before I can face you being mad at me."

She scowled. "I told you. I need to go and work for him ..." She jerked her head at the spot where Spider had been standing. "What the ..."

Oscar smirked. He couldn't help it. "Come on, Grace, you can't blame him."

She drew in a deep breath, looking as if she might explode, then slowly let it out, looking defeated and much more tired than Oscar had realized she was. "Did you say something about a beer and some meatloaf?"

He smiled and slung his arm around her shoulders. "I sure did. Let's go eat."

Chapter Eighteen

By the time they were settled into a booth at Gavin's, Grace felt like Spider might be right. She was in danger of keeling over from exhaustion. Once Gavin had brought their beers, Oscar reached across the table and took hold of her hand. "You look wiped out."

"I am."

"It's been a long week, we've achieved a lot, but it's been twice as hard for you. You've had to go work for Harry all day."

"Tell me something I don't know."

He smiled. "That I'll be glad when you're finished there."

She pursed her lips. She wanted to yell at him, but she knew he meant well; he just didn't understand. "I'll probably be just as tired then, I won't be working all day, I'll be pounding the streets looking for work instead."

"You don't need to do that."

She scowled. "I don't have a big fat savings account I can live on for a while. This is me you're talking to remember, not one of your other friends."

He smiled but didn't say anything.

"What?"

"You think of us as friends?"

"Yeah. I do." She'd been able to come to terms with that over the course of the last week. At first, she'd thought he would disappear after they had sex; that was all he wanted women for. She knew now she'd been wrong about that. He'd stepped in to save the center. He'd spent every moment she could spare with her. They worked well together at the center, and they worked even better together in bed every night afterward. He'd been as good to her as anyone had ever been, and that had helped her relax around him. She'd let him into her inner circle—which was very small. She was under no illusions about a relationship with him—she'd told the truth when she'd told his mom that neither of them was looking for one of those—but she had come to see him, and to trust him, as a friend. A thought struck her. Maybe his smile was amusement at her assumption. "Don't you?"

He shrugged. "Maybe."

Oh. Her heart sank, and a ball of disappointment settled in her stomach. He didn't then. Maybe she was just a perk of the project. He'd told her he threw himself one hundred percent into everything he did. Maybe she was just one element of the center that he was doing well.

Gavin returned with their meatloaf and gave them an inquiring look. Oscar shook his head slightly, and Gavin backed away without a word.

"I'm sorry." Grace had recovered enough to get past the awkwardness. He didn't owe her a damned thing. He certainly didn't owe her friendship. "I really am beat." She dropped her gaze to her plate and set to work on her food.

They ate in silence for a while until Oscar set his fork down and looked at her. "I don't know if this is the wrong time to bring this up, but how would you feel about working at the center?"

She met his gaze. "What do you think I've been doing?"

"I mean, taking a job, with a salary. Becoming an employee of the nonprofit."

She stared at him for a long a moment, then carried on eating while she thought about it. The part of her that had, at various points over the last few weeks, dreamed about being in a real relationship with him, railed against the idea. She couldn't take a job from him. She couldn't be dependent on him for her living. It'd be all wrong. Another part of her, the part that had ensured her survival in a cruel world was nodding. It made sense. She knew how to run the place. She did it well. It'd give her the time to dedicate to making the place a success. She'd love to spend her days serving the community and making sure they were taken care of—especially if it meant she'd be able to take care of herself by getting paid for it. Eventually, she looked up. "Have you brought this up with the others yet?"

"No. I wanted to ask you first."

"Well, I think we should establish a real committee, and I think you should run it by them."

"And if they agree, you'll do it?"

"Yeah. It makes sense." It really did make sense, even though to her it meant that she and Oscar would never have any kind of relationship. Not a real one. She'd keep sleeping with him until he lost interest. But he didn't even see her as a friend. And even if he wanted to—which she now knew was a crazy idea—he could never be her boyfriend and her boss.

He smiled, but he still looked concerned. "Are you sure you're okay with it?"

"If you are." She wondered if he might say something—about the two of them—but he didn't.

When they got back to his place, he backed her up against the door as soon as they went inside. She was tired, and she was sad that her little fantasy about them being friends really was nothing more than a fantasy. The feel of his arms around her and the weight of his body leaning against her still felt like coming home. She needed to get over that. Whatever that pull between them was, it obviously meant nothing to him. Still, she wrapped her arms around him and pulled him close. Wanting to feel for a moment that she belonged somewhere, that she belonged here, with him. Even though she knew it wasn't true, the warm feeling still washed over her, and she clung to him.

His hands which had been roving over her back and her ass stilled. He sensed the change in her, and she felt it in him too. He wrapped his arms around her and hugged her close to his chest. "I wish I understood you, Grace."

She let out a bitter little laugh, which sounded a lot like a sob. "Ditto."

He leaned back and hooked his thumb under her chin, forcing her to look up into her eyes.

"Did I do something wrong, Gracie?"

Her breath caught in her throat. Spider called her Gracie, Terry called her Gracie, lots of people did but hearing him say it was too much. That feeling that filled the air between them that filled her up whenever he was close threatened to overflow and engulf her. He sounded so tender, so caring. She had to remember that it was no doubt just part of his repertoire. She shook her head. "No. You really didn't."

She could tell he didn't believe her, but he let it go.

"Can we just go to bed?"

He took her hand and led her through to his bedroom. She was amazed how quickly she'd felt at home here. She, the girl who'd slept in alleys and under bridges had adapted, without issue, to sleeping in a bedroom that was bigger than Louise's entire apartment. She no longer found it strange to walk on the marble floor or to get ready in his dressing room in the morning. She just hoped that her transition back to her own reality would go as quickly and easily once this was over.

He sat down on the edge of the bed and drew her to him. "Do you want to just go to sleep?"

She nodded. She didn't, but if he was suggesting it, then he couldn't be that hot for her tonight. It was hardly surprising; she knew she must look like crap. She was so tired.

When they were both in bed, he turned out the light and rolled over to kiss her cheek. "I care about you, Grace. I hope you know that."

She held her breath for a moment. She didn't even know what that meant to him. He didn't see her as a friend, but he cared about her? Maybe she was a charity project to him, like the center. She bit her lip to stop herself thinking that way. It was stupid. He meant well, that was all she needed to know.

She kissed his cheek and looked at him, glad for the darkness so he couldn't see her face. "I care about you, too."

He wrapped his arm around her and held her close. Once again, the warmth of contentment swept through her. How could she feel so close and connected when he felt nothing? Well, he cared for her.

The warmth of something more than contentment began to build between her legs. She might be exhausted, but she wasn't made of stone. His strong arm was around her, her breasts were pushed up against his chest, and she was sure that if she edged forward a little, she'd feel the heat of his thick hard shaft.

She couldn't resist. She did edge forward—and she was right. She brought her hand up and caressed his face, then threaded her fingers through his hair.

"I thought you were too tired," he murmured, even though she could feel him growing bigger as she ran her fingers down his neck.

"So did I, but I want you so much. I'll never get to sleep unless we ..."

He propped himself up on one elbow and ran a finger down her cheek. Then he traced her jawline and continued down her throat and between her breasts. "How about you lie back and let me do the work then?"

She smiled. "It'd be my pleasure."

"I'll make sure of it."

~ ~ ~

Oscar knew he could give her all the pleasure she could handle, physically. He'd hoped that they were getting closer, too, but she'd gone cold on him tonight, and he thought he knew why. At dinner when she'd said she thought of him as a friend, he'd screwed up. She'd asked if he thought of her as a friend and he hadn't wanted to say yes. He'd started to think of her as more than a friend. He was now convinced that his mom was right—that Grace was his person. The one he was supposed to be with. It was so far out of left field that it made him edgy, but he knew it was true.

His attempt at letting her know that he thought of her as more than a friend had backfired on him. His answer of maybe had pissed her off. That was the only explanation. She'd changed after that. Maybe she'd felt like he was pressuring her. He didn't know. All he knew was that she hadn't been receptive.

He cupped her cheek in his hand and looked down at her. It was dark enough that he couldn't see her face clearly, but he knew she was looking back into his eyes. Maybe with time, she'd learn to love him? He wasn't about to give up. He'd slow down, win her over, do whatever it took.

Right now, he had the opportunity to love her, and he wasn't going to waste another minute stuck inside his head. If he had his way, he'd love her hard every night until she loved him back.

He walked his fingers down over her ribs and then slid them over the curve of her belly and between her legs. As he stroked her, she sighed, and her arms came up around his neck. "Fuck me, Oscar."

He was glad she couldn't see his smirk in the dark. He loved that she was so blunt, and he was only too happy to oblige. She was already wet for him, and his cock was straining to be inside her, He positioned himself above her, and her arms came up around his back.

"Hard," she breathed.

He closed his eyes and clenched his jaw, wanting to take it slow, to be tender. Her fingernails sank into his ass, and he gasped as his hips thrust hard and he plunged deep, making her gasp with him.

She grazed her nails up his back and then back down before digging them hard into his ass again. It ignited him, and he lost control, going harder and faster, plunging deep inside her as she gasped beneath him. She brought her legs up and wrapped them around his back, allowing him to go even deeper. He was pounding into her, and she was urging him faster and faster. Some part of his mind became lucid enough for a moment to realize that she was making this all about him. No. He'd promised her pleasure. He slid his hand between them and circled her clit with his thumb. She groaned, and as her inner muscles clenched around him. He knew he didn't need to do anything with it, just the extra pressure was enough. He found his rhythm again, each thrust of his hips burying his cock deeper and pressing his thumb against her most sensitive spot. Her groans grew louder. "Oscar! I ..." He didn't want to leave her with enough breath to talk. He picked up his pace, and the tension building at the bottom of his spine began to ripple outward. The ripples became a tidal wave as Grace's orgasm took her. Her muscles tightened and drew him in, milking him for all he had. As his mind spun away, that was the only thought he could hold onto—he wanted to give her all he had.

He wanted to love her with his body, his mind, and his whole self.

When they finally lay spent, he rested his head on her shoulder with a smile on his face. Now he knew what his next challenge was. He was going to win her love. He was finally ready to admit to himself that he was falling in love with her, and he was going to make Grace Evans love him right back—no matter what it took. He pressed his lips to the side of her neck, tempted to whisper those three little words right there and then. Instead, he rolled onto the bed in surprise as she pushed him off and got out. He sighed as she padded to the bathroom. He'd get used to her ways, and maybe as she got used to him, she'd soften up a little.

When she came back, he could tell she was staring up at the ceiling. He moved closer and wrapped an arm around her. "You okay?"

"Mm-hmm."

He knew she was worn out. Tomorrow, he'd make sure she had a relaxing day. They'd do something fun, and he'd make sure she got some rest.

Chapter Nineteen

The next morning Grace woke late. It took her a minute to realize that she was in Oscar's bed—but he wasn't. She sighed. She could get used to this if she allowed herself. But there was no point even thinking about whether she could allow herself to. She probably would find a way—if Oscar wanted her to, but he didn't. She remembered the smirk on his face last night at dinner when she'd asked if he thought of her as a friend. His reply had been, Maybe. Maybe was a long way from yes, as far as she was concerned. She rolled onto her side. She should get up, but his bed was so comfortable, she didn't want to. She sighed again. Maybe it was just because she was so tired that she felt so emotional. She didn't normally let her feelings get the better of her—she couldn't afford to—but right now she was sad. She was feeling sorry for herself. She wished he'd come back to bed and hold her, make love to her, and tell her everything was going to be okay, that he did see her as a friend and that maybe someday he could see her as something more than that.

She sat up. Unfortunately, she lived in the real world. There were no fairy tale endings for girls like her, and she was okay with that. She wouldn't want to be a needy, dependent little girl anyway. She was strong and she was tough and she could make it on her own. She always had. She bit the inside of her lip at the tired little voice in her head that said she always had because she'd always had to, and it would be nice to have someone to lean on, to share life with. Maybe it would, and maybe somewhere down the line, she'd meet someone who would fit that description. Oscar wasn't someone to lean on or share with. Oscar was a guy who had fun and moved on. She needed to get real and get back to enjoying what was on offer before he did move on.

The door opened, and he peeked around it.

"You're awake."

She smiled. "I am. Sorry, I slept in, I must have needed it."

"Don't be sorry. I'm glad you could. Are you ready to get up yet, or do you want to rest some more?"

That familiar warm feeling washed over her. Even though she knew there was no future in it, it still felt so good that he cared about her. She held her arms out to him. Why not? She knew she wasn't the softest woman on earth, but only because she'd grown so used to keeping her walls up and keeping people out. He came to her with a smile and closed his arms around her. She rested her head against his chest; she couldn't help it. That connection they shared felt so strong. She couldn't deny that she felt like she belonged right here in his arms. Tears pricked her eyes. He might not feel the same way, but then he didn't need to. He was giving her more than she'd ever known just by being here. It didn't need to be his burden. She could live this little fantasy by herself.

He stroked her hair away from her face, just like he'd done that first morning they'd met. The electricity still zapped through, but it wasn't just a physical desire. It zapped straight to her heart, too, and in that moment, she understood that her heart would break the day he said goodbye.

"Are you okay, Gracie?"

The tears began to flow. She couldn't remember the last time she'd cried. Crying didn't help anything, but that knowledge couldn't stop her now. It came out in big gasping sobs.

He hugged her closer to his chest and kissed the top of her head. He didn't ask questions, and he didn't get up and walk away, he just held her and let her get it all out.

When it finally subsided, she looked up at him. She felt like she must have totally blown it, no guy wanted a sobbing woman in his bed. She knew that wasn't the case though. She could feel how much he cared. "I'm sorry," she mumbled, then sniffed and started to swipe at her face.

He caught her chin between his finger and thumb and made her look up into his eyes.

"Please tell me."

She wanted to ask, tell him what? But she knew, and she didn't want to push him away. Instead, she shrugged sadly. "I guess I'm over tired."

He nodded and waited. They both knew that was the beginning of an explanation, not the end.

"Okay. I'm going to tell you, even though it'll probably mean goodbye."

His look of concern turned into something else. If she had to find a word for it, she'd say he looked scared, but that couldn't be right. "Go ahead," was all he said.

"Let me start by saying none of this is your fault. It's all on me."

His long, strong fingers tightened around hers. "What is?"

She blew out a big sigh and tried to compose herself. He was a good guy; she owed him honesty and she had to get on with it. "I care about you too much."

His eyebrows came down. Shit. He wasn't going to like this, but she'd started now.

"I'm sure you've been put in this position dozens of times, but it's not somewhere I've ever been before. I know I don't mean much to you. You made it clear last night when you said you don't even see us as friends. But I care about you. You make me feel things I haven't felt before. I keep wishing that this, what we have, what we're doing, could last." He started to speak, but she put a finger to his lips. "Don't. Please. You don't need to say anything. I know this isn't your fault, you've been nothing but honest with me. I couldn't help it though. For the first time in my life, you've made me feel that I belong somewhere." She stopped and gave him a sad smile. "You make me feel like I belong with you, but I know I don't."

"Grace, I …"

She shook her head and wriggled out of his arms. "There's nothing left to say. I'm going to go take a shower and let you make of that what you will. While I'm in there, you can decide what you want to do with what I've told you."

She couldn't figure out the look on his face, but she went into the bathroom and closed the door. She'd done it. She'd been honest with him. She didn't expect anything from him in return. She hoped he wouldn't be so freaked out that he'd show her the door, but he might be. She could deal with that. She knew him well enough to know that it wouldn't affect his involvement in the center. He was doing that for himself, not for her.

~ ~ ~

Oscar sat and stared at the bathroom door in amazement. Had he just imagined that? He shook his head as if to clear it. Had she really just told him that she felt like she belonged with him. Had Grace—tough Grace, Grace the hard-ass, just sat and sobbed in his arms? He nodded. She really had. Damn!

He sucked in a deep breath and slowly blew it out. And what was he going to do with that? His first instinct was to follow her into the bathroom, join her in the shower and show her just how much he loved her. He instinctively ran his thumb over his lips as he smiled. No. There'd be plenty of occasions he could make love to her. What he needed to do first was show her that he loved her with words and gestures. He got to his feet. He was going to make her breakfast, and while they ate, he was going to tell her that he'd fallen in love with her. He got to his feet. Damn. It was hard to believe this was happening. Only last night he'd thought he'd have a long road ahead. He'd planned to earn her trust and hopefully someday her love. Now it sounded like she'd already given him both. He made his way back to the kitchen with a big grin on his face. Now he really had something to throw himself into.

After half an hour, he went back to see if she was nearly ready. She wasn't in the bedroom or the dressing room, so he knocked on the bathroom door. Nothing. He frowned. "Are you in there, Grace?" It didn't sound like it. He opened the door and pushed it open. She wasn't.

He ran a hand through his hair and stared around in confusion. Where the hell was she? He returned to the kitchen, checked in the den, then went outside onto the terrace. There was no sign of her. He went back to the bedroom and then he saw it—a note lying on his pillow.

Sorry. I shouldn't have embarrassed us both like that. I won't make this awkward—for either of us. Have a great weekend. I'll see you at the center on Monday. We can pretend this never happened—please?

G x

Oscar read the note through twice. He didn't get it. How had she embarrassed anyone? Where had she gone? How had she sneaked out—and why?

He carried the note to the front door and stared up the driveway. He couldn't see her, but then he didn't expect to. He went back inside and then stopped dead in the hallway when realization dawned. He'd been so happy to hear how she felt about him. He was looking forward to them being together now they both knew how they felt. But he'd overlooked one kind of major detail. He hadn't had the chance to tell her how he felt. What a total dumbass! She had no clue how he felt. He'd tried to protest when she'd talked about him not even seeing her as a friend. He didn't just see her as a friend—he wanted her to be so much more than that. But she didn't know that. He'd stayed quiet at her insistence and let her say her piece, but she'd gone before he'd had the chance to do the same. Damn.

He grabbed the keys for the Range Rover from the hook. He had to find her. She couldn't have gone far. He knew there were no bus stops around here.

~ ~ ~

Grace got out of the cab in front of the center. That had been a dumb thing to do. Cab fares weren't cheap, and she was only just scraping by. She hadn't discussed with Oscar what her new job at the center might pay. It was funny; she didn't even question that he might not give her the job anymore. It may have been dumb to tell him how she felt, but she didn't regret it. It was only fair. She knew she'd been moody and weird around him a few times—all because she wanted more from him. Telling him had been the right thing to do. He had a right to know. Running out of there hadn't been one of the wisest things she'd ever done, but she'd had to.

She'd thought about it as she stood in the shower letting the hot water run down over her. She'd done what she needed to, but she hadn't considered how awkward that might be for him. He was only looking to get laid. He'd admitted that was a goal he set every day. She didn't want to make his life difficult, so she'd left. He shouldn't have to face her and feel embarrassed. He could go about his business, go to his club tonight if he wanted to—and get laid. She shuddered. The thought of him with another woman. No. She couldn't let her mind go there.

She let herself in through the front door of the center and smiled as she looked around. It was busy, as it always was on a Saturday. Little kids were running around. The oldies were holding court in the cafeteria. A bunch of vets were watching TV. She spotted TJ amongst them and turned away—only to see Terry sitting there.

"What are you doing here, Gracie?"

"Same as I always do. What are you doing here?"

He chuckled. "Okay, now I know something's up. Why so defensive?"

"I'm not."

"Yes, you are. Where's Oscar?"

"Why would I know?"

He shook his head and scowled. "Why do you run away from anything good in your life?"

"I don't know what you're talking about. I don't."

"I think you do."

Grace shook her head. "I really don't. I haven't had many good things in my life, Terry. The few I've had have either been taken away from me, or I'm still clinging on tight." She relaxed a little as she realized the truth of that. "I have this place and you and Spider and Louise. I'm hanging on to all of you."

"And what about Oscar?"

"He's not in my life."

"Only because you ran out on him."

Her heart started to pound. "And what do you know about it?"

"He just called, wanting to know if you were here. I told him, no, but he asked me to let him know if you show up."

"Well, I'm asking you not to."

"Sorry, Gracie. I gave him my word."

"Okay, bye then."

She turned around. She didn't need Oscar chasing her down here. There was no need for it. She'd see him on Monday. Hopefully, then, it would be a little less embarrassing for both of them.

"Why don't you want to hear what he has to say?"

"Because, Terry, I made a fool of myself."

"I don't think so. I think you should wait till he gets here, listen to him."

"There's no point. He doesn't want me, and I like him too much."

"He does want you, you stubborn girl. Why won't you see that? I can see it; hell, everyone can see it. Everyone except you. Any other girl would be thrilled that a guy like him had fallen in love with her. You? You're too busy fighting for survival to even notice."

"What do you mean? You of all people know what it's like to have to fight to survive. I thought you'd understand." Grace was angry. She'd never have expected Terry to turn on her. She'd raised her voice and people were looking at them. She stalked to the back door and let herself out. Terry followed and waited until she'd taken up her perch on the wall before he spoke again.

"I'm sorry, Gracie. I don't want to upset you, but you need to hear it. You're so used to believing that you have to fight for everything that you haven't noticed that something amazing has landed in your lap."

Grace scowled at him. "I have realized. We're saving this place. That's amazing. And okay, I'll admit it. Oscar and me seeing each other—that's been amazing. I have noticed it, and I am grateful for this good thing that's happened to me. I've tried to make the most of it, but I want more, and I know that's stupid, okay?

Terry shook his head. "I'll tell you what's stupid, shall I?"

Grace nodded sullenly. She knew he was going to.

"You've gotten so used to surviving that you can't see beyond it. I'm not criticizing you. I'm trying to help. I see you doing the same thing I did."

"What do you mean."

"Remember that first morning we met, and you gave me your coffee?"

Grace nodded.

"It threw me. I'd spent the night sleeping in here because it was too cold outside. I'd survived. That's all I was trying to do. Then you gave me coffee, and I didn't know what to do with it. I didn't need coffee, I didn't even want coffee. Coffee was more than I thought I deserved at that point." Terry stopped and stared off into space. "What I'm trying to say, Gracie is that life has given us a lot of lemons—you and me—and we've gotten pretty good at making lemonade."

She gave him a grudging smile. She could agree with that.

"But that's not all there is. I learned it when you encouraged me to keep coming back here. Yeah. I could make it through the night without freezing to death, and I could scavenge enough to eat, but there's so much more to life. There's friendship and community—and there's love like I've found here." He smiled. "You're in the same trap I was."

"It's not a trap though. I'm proud of myself. I'm proud of what I'm doing for this place, what I've achieved so far."

Terry shook his head. "You should be proud of yourself. Like I said, you've gotten pretty good at making lemonade, but that doesn't mean your story should end with lemonade. This Oscar—he's crazy about you. We all see it; we all know it, but you think he's so far out of your league you're not even open to the idea. Gracie, right now, life is offering you champagne and strawberries, and you're turning them down because you only know how to make lemonade."

Grace's eyes filled with tears and a big lump formed in her throat. She slid down from the wall and crouched beside Terry's wheelchair. "I love you, Terry."

"Love you, too, Gracie," he croaked.

Chapter Twenty

Oscar couldn't find a spot to park anywhere near the center. When he finally found a space, he ran the rest of the way. Terry had called to say Grace was here, but he wouldn't be surprised if she left again. He needed to find her, needed to tell her how he felt.

He pushed the front door open and stood there, staring wildly around. No sign of her. Damn. TJ spotted him and came over. "What's up?"

"Is she here?"

"She was. She went out back with Terry. What's going on?"

"No time to explain."

TJ smiled and gripped his shoulder. "It's finally come down to that then? Go get your girl."

Oscar nodded and strode over to the back door. That was what he was going to do. He was going to get his girl. She was his person. His mom had been right.

The door opened just before he reached it and Terry came wheeling out. He nodded when he saw Oscar and gave him an encouraging smile. He didn't say anything, but he held the door open.

Oscar took a deep breath and went outside. She was so damned beautiful. She took his breath away every time. She met his gaze, and he held a hand out to her. She nodded and slid down from the wall where she'd been sitting.

"Grace, I ..."

"I'm sorry I ran out on you."

He smiled and buttoned her lips between his finger and thumb. Her eyes widened, but he shook his head. "I need to talk. If you'd let me talk earlier, we could have saved ourselves a lot of trouble. I'm sorry, I was an idiot."

She tried to speak again, but he smiled and squeezed her lips tighter. "It's my turn. I was so stunned by what you said earlier."

Her eyes darted away from his.

"Listen, I need to make sure I spell this out. I don't want there to be any chance whatsoever that you misunderstand me. Last night when you asked if I thought of you as a friend, I said maybe. I didn't say yes because I'd like you to be so much more than a friend."

She stared at him. If he only had the look on her face as his guide, he'd be tempted to shut the hell up, but he knew better. He also had what she'd told him this morning about how she felt. So he pushed on. It was time to put his heart on the line. "What I'm trying to say is that I love you. I've fallen head over heels in love with you."

She jerked her head back, freeing her lips. "What?!"

"You heard me. I love you."

She stared at him. "You do? But I'm not ... You're ..."

He slid his arms around her waist and drew her to him. "Don't, don't even go there. None of it matters. I love you. I know you care about me ..."

She nodded. "I love you, too, but …"

"No buts. Stop trying to complicate it. I love you, you love me. Nothing else matters. Between us, we can overcome anything."

She nodded. "I guess we can. But isn't this just a short-term thing for you, enjoy it while it lasts and then …"

He shook his head. "Nope. You don't get rid of me that easily. This is for keeps. I never thought I wanted anyone for keeps, but I want you. You're my person."

"Your person?"

He chuckled. "Yeah. It's what my mom said."

Grace raised an eyebrow.

"She said sometimes you meet someone, and you just know."

"Know what?"

"That they're your person, your one and only, your love, the one you're meant to spend your life with."

Her eyes filled with tears and he dropped a kiss on the end of her nose. "Don't cry, Gracie."

"They're happy tears. I never thought I'd hear you talk like that—about anyone, let alone about me."

"Neither did I." He nodded. "But you're the one, Gracie. I want to love you for the rest of my life. You and me, this, us, we're my next challenge. The most important challenge of my life."

She smiled. "I can be challenging."

He chuckled. "Believe me, I know."

She pushed at his shoulder. "Aren't you supposed to say nice things and deny it?"

He shook his head. "I don't think so. Part of what I love about you is that you're so honest and you love that I'm so honest. I love you because you're real."

She nodded. "Yeah. There's no denying that."

"I wouldn't want to."

She frowned. "But what do you want? What does this mean? Where do we go from here?"

"Wherever we want to take it. I'd like you to move in with me."

Her eyes narrowed. "I can afford my own place."

"I know you can, but that's not the point, is it?"

She shook her head. "I guess I need to get over that, don't I? Always jumping on the defensive."

"It'd be nice, but I don't expect miracles straight away."

"Good."

The door swung open, and they both turned to see who was there. Oscar laughed at the sight of TJ, Spider, Louise, and Terry all huddled in the doorway.

Grace chuckled beside him. "Yes, can we help you?"

Spider grinned. "Err, I wondered if you want to work a shift at the coffee shop this afternoon."

Grace tensed, but Oscar knew what he was getting at. "Sorry," he answered for her, "my girlfriend is busy this afternoon."

She turned to stare up at him. If they were going to do this, he was sure that there'd be many more moments like this. She thought he was dictating what she did, and she felt like she needed to work for the money. He didn't want either of those things to be true. He met her gaze and waited. His heart buzzed in his chest when her expression softened, and she smiled. "Yeah, sorry Spider."

Oscar tightened his arm around her waist, feeling as if they'd just succeeded in the first challenge they'd face as a couple.

Spider grinned at him. "No worries, no worries at all."

~ ~ ~

They had dinner at Oscar's. He'd told Grace he'd love it if she thought of it as her place, too, but she knew that would a take a long time—if ever. He'd taken a call about some problem at the club. This was the second Saturday night in a row that he hadn't been at Six. She'd thought of it as just a playground for him, but it seemed he did have some managerial responsibility for the place.

She picked up her glass of wine and took it outside onto the terrace to admire the view. Could she see herself living here? She smiled. She could. All because of Oscar. She'd live here for him—not off him. Since he'd told her that he loved her, she was seeing things in a whole new light. Knowing that he felt that way about her explained so many of his actions. He was still an arrogant prick. She smiled. She hoped he always would be, but the sweet guy, the one who showed so much concern—that wasn't some other version of him—it was simply a man in love. In love with her! That changed everything.

He'd talked about her moving in here and she would. One thing she knew about love—what she'd seen at least, was that it never worked out if one or both people were holding back, waiting for it to fail. She was going to do the same as Oscar. She was going to throw herself into it with all that she was. She'd give up her room at Louise's; she'd give up her shifts at the coffee shop. She took a big gulp of her wine—she was even going to take the job as the center manager, which meant Oscar would be paying her wages. That was a tough pill to swallow, but as he'd said, she was real, a realist. She'd never before had the luxury of turning down a job because she didn't like the owner—their money was as good as anyone else's. In this case, she happened to be in love with the guy who'd be paying her. She'd decided that she had to lay that aside—see it like he'd said in the beginning, as two separate issues. There was the guy who'd come in to help the center out financially, and then there was the guy and the girl who'd met in the elevator, and they still had unfinished business. She smiled. She hoped they always would.

Oscar came out to find her. "Sorry, that took a while."

"That's okay, it's work. You have to take care of it."

He smiled. "Why is it I expect to hear that from you about late nights at the center."

"Because you know me."

"And I love you."

She went to him and slid her arms around his waist. "I'm still finding that hard to believe."

He closed his hands around her ass. "I'd be happy to prove it to you—all night long if you like."

She laughed. "I'm sure you would."

He went back to the patio doors and held his hand out for her to follow. When she reached him, he took her hand and winked. "Just don't say those two little words?"

Grace raised an eyebrow. "I thought you liked it when I tell you to fuck me?"

He groaned and shook his head. "I do. I like it way too much, but tonight I want to make love to you."

Grace's heart melted. She would never have guessed that the guy she met in the elevator, Big Cat, the arrogant prick, was capable of wanting to make love—let alone to her. She took his hand and followed him through to the bedroom knowing that this was the beginning of a new chapter in their life.

~ ~ ~

By the time Grace officially started work at the center, she and Oscar had been living together for a whole week. They'd had their challenges, but no major roadblocks so far. This morning she was waiting for him to finish getting ready so they could go.

"Come on," she said when he reached the bottom of the stairs. "I don't want to be late for my first day."

He laughed. "Would it be okay with you if I get a cup of coffee first?"

She pointed to the entry table where two travel mugs sat. "You think I'd force you out the door without coffee?"

He went to her and slid his arms around her waist. "You're more domesticated than I give you credit for. You're going to make a good little wifey someday, aren't you?"

She pursed her lips and looked up into his eyes. "Not if you keep up with that kind of talk, I'm not."

The words had come out before he'd had chance to consider their implications. He held her gaze. "And if I quit talking like that. Would you consider it?"

Her eyes widened. "We're going to be late. Let's go."

He knew her well enough by now. He knew she sidestepped anything she didn't want to deal with immediately. As he drove them to the center, part of him was grateful. Did he want to get married yet? He wasn't sure. Did he want to get married at all? Yes. The answer surprised him; it came so swiftly and with such certainty. He wanted to marry Grace Evans. He wanted her to have the kind of life she'd never known. He wanted to give her a home and security. He wanted her to always feel like he was where she belonged in the world. It'd touched his heart when she'd said that, and it was important to him that he should never let her down.

He shot a glance over at her. She had a notebook on her lap and was scribbling away in it. She'd been doing that all weekend. She was excited about finally being able to give attention to the center full time.

"Wouldn't it be easier to use a laptop?"

She pursed her lips but didn't reply.

At first, he thought she was concentrating and didn't want the interruption, then it dawned on him. She didn't have a laptop. He'd have to get her one. He could say it went with the job. No. He smiled to himself. He couldn't take the easy way out; she needed one. He was going to get her one, and if she was going to get mad at him about it, then let her. He knew how independent she was, but she was going to have to let her realistic side come to the fore on some things. If she was going to be his wife, she'd have to get used to him buying her things—things that she needed and things that she wanted. His wife! The thought didn't freak him out; in fact, he was starting to think that maybe he was ready. He glanced over at her again. Grace Davenport. He wanted to laugh. He sounded like a schoolgirl.

~ ~ ~

The first day of her new job was better than Grace had ever hoped. It wasn't easy, she was going to be crazy busy for the next couple of months, and it was never going to be a cushy job, but it was everything Grace wanted to do. She finally got to devote her time and energy to the place. And she had the resources to make things happen.

The guys had built her a little office. They'd created a work space for her by partitioning off the corner by the pantry. She'd never imagined having an office before. She loved it. It even had a window, so she could look out and see what was going on. It was late afternoon, and the kids were starting to trickle in. Soon the young moms would leave, and in a couple of hours, the vets would start to drift in. She knew the rhythm of the place so well. She just wished she could do as much for the life of every person who came in here as … she nodded, she had to admit it … as Oscar had done for her. Damn. She loved that man.

He wasn't here this afternoon. He'd had to go over to the club and catch up there. She wondered how long it would be before he found himself a new challenge. He was invested in the center, and she believed he would continue to be, but she knew that he needed a new project. It made sense. They'd turn the center around together, she had faith in that, but the center was her purpose in life. Oscar wasn't the kind of guy who had a single purpose. He climbed mountains, and once he conquered one, he moved on to the next.

She chewed the end of her pencil. This morning he'd talked about her being his wife. She couldn't help the smile that plastered itself across her face. She'd love to! But she wasn't sure it was a great idea. He kept telling her she was it. She was the one he wanted for life. She was his person. But this was all so new. She believed he meant what he said, but no one ever knew how they'd feel in the future. Would he still feel the same way in six months—a year? Given his track record, she doubted it.

Did she want to get married and take that risk? She didn't know. She didn't want to end up divorced. Her life had been a series of temporary situations, and she didn't want to go into a marriage only to find that it, too, was temporary. Living together was one thing—there was no expectation of forever. Getting married, to her at least, was meant to be forever, and she didn't think she could handle setting herself up for the heartbreak of it not being.

She looked up at the sound of a knock on her door. It was TJ. She liked him a lot.

"Come on in, take a seat."

"Thanks." He sat down across the desk from her and smiled. Johnny and Jean sure had produced some good-looking boys. While Oscar was the cocky and outgoing kind of gorgeous, TJ was quieter, the more intense, broody kind. He was a heart-stopper, no question about it, but Grace knew that his waters ran deep. Grace realized she was smiling at him but hadn't actually spoken yet. "What's up?"

"I wanted to see how your first day's going. I know you've waited a long time for this, and I didn't want the day to go by without us marking the occasion."

Damn. He was sweet too? She'd never noticed before. "Thanks, TJ. That means a lot. There's a hell of a lot of work to do—and thank you for everything you've already done. You've mended a lot of fences that I broke over the years."

He grinned. "That's okay. It's done me good."

She nodded. She didn't know what his story was, but she knew he'd been through a lot. It seemed the center had become as much of a lifeline for him as it had for so many of the others. A thought occurred to her. "Do you plan to stick around?"

He shrugged. "I've been waiting to see what you think."

She smiled. "I'd love it. I'd love to make it official. I can't do it all, and as we both know, you have strengths that compliment my weaknesses."

He smiled. "I wouldn't have brought that up."

"Yeah, wise man, but we need to be honest about it."

"I guess we do. So, what I'm thinking is I'd like to set up a program for the vets. I'll help out with anything else you need, of course, but I think I can do a lot of good with the vets—for them and me."

"I agree. It works perfectly."

"Great. I know you've got a bunch of meetings set up this week, so I'll draw something up that I can lay out for you. I'd like to be here full time from now on."

Grace nodded. She liked the idea, but she didn't know how to bring up the matter of whether he'd need a salary. She'd been surprised when she learned that Oscar had made his own money. She had to wonder how TJ had fared. She didn't know how to bring it up.

He made a face, and she waited. "I wanted to ask how you feel about me being on the board. I don't have the same kind of money Oscar does, but I can be another source of funding."

Apparently, Grace didn't hide her surprise very well.

"I don't just get a pension. I made some smart investments early on."

She raised an eyebrow. She wouldn't have imagined TJ as the investing type.

He laughed. "I loaned my brother all the money I had when he started his first company."

Grace had to laugh with him. "Wow! That did turn out to be a smart investment."

"Yeah. I knew there was very little risk, though. I mean. He's Oscar."

Grace nodded. Could she have that much faith in him? Should she.

TJ met her gaze. "What's troubling you?"

She blew out a sigh. "I love him. You know that."

He nodded.

"Could you ever see him getting married?"

"Before you? No. Now? I'm just waiting for the two of you to name the day."

Grace looked up and saw Oscar standing in the doorway. Had he heard all of that? His smile said he had.

"I got finished early at the club. I wondered if you wanted to celebrate tonight?"

"You mean go out for dinner?"

He shook his head. "No. I meant bring dinner here—for everyone."

He jerked his head, and she and TJ both went to join him in the doorway. Grace had to smile at the sight of a whole line of caterers walking in. Terry was wheeling along beside them issuing directions as they set up what looked like a banquet that would feed the whole neighborhood.

TJ grinned at them. "I'll go help set up."

Grace went to Oscar and slid her arms around his waist. "Thank you. You're not only changing my life for the better, but you're also changing all of theirs, too."

He slung his arm around her shoulder and hugged her into his side. "I'm the one who should be saying thank you. You're the one who's changed my life for the better. I'll admit that at first, I wanted to be the knight in shining armor who rode in to save the day. In the end though, you and this place, you've saved me."

Grace smiled up at him. "How about we agree that we both saved each other?"

He nodded. "I believe we did."

Grace leaned her head against his shoulder. That feeling of warmth washed through her. She'd spent her whole life longing for a place to belong, and now she knew she'd finally found it, here, by his side;

Epilogue

A few months later

Montana was so beautiful. Oscar had brought Grace up here every weekend they could spare, and she loved it. The mountains and the wide-open spaces were so different from the city where she'd spent her whole life so far, and there was no denying that the lifestyle was entirely different from what she'd lived so far. She smiled. She'd adapted quickly and easily to it; if she was honest, this life suited her, and she hoped it would be a big part of their future.

She stood on the deck of Oscar's house and looked down at the yard by the river. Dozens of people were milling around. It was Johnny's birthday, and Oscar and his brothers had wanted to throw a party for their dad.

Grace smiled as she spotted Terry sitting beside Oscar's uncle, Seymour Davenport. The two of them were deep in conversation about something. She shook her head. Terry hadn't been so sure about coming, but TJ had talked him into it, and she was glad. Like her, he'd always wanted to see Yellowstone, and TJ was going to take him and Spider and Louise down there tomorrow. It was strange for her to see her friends in this setting—strange, but good. Her two worlds were very different, but they were merging into one more easily than she would have imagined. Terry, the guy who'd lived on the streets for years, was lost in conversation with Seymour Davenport, a man who Grace had only previously known as a billionaire mentioned on the news occasionally. Spider was talking to Chance, Hope Davenport's husband, who looked a lot more at home up here in the mountains dressed in butt-hugging Wranglers and a cowboy hat than he had the last time Grace had seen him, in a suit at Six.

She scanned the crowd and chuckled when she spotted Louise. TJ had been fending her off ever since that night she'd invited herself into the limo. It looked like his struggle was over; for now, at least. She'd transferred her attention to the third brother, Reid. Grace wasn't sure what to make of him. He was quiet, and from what Oscar had told her, somewhat reclusive, but when they'd been introduced, he'd given Grace a warm smile and had a friendly air about him. She was looking forward to getting to know him.

"How are you doing, Grace?"

She turned to smile at Jean who'd come to lean on the deck rail beside her.

"I'm great, thanks. How about you?"

"I couldn't be happier. My husband is loving his birthday and having so many friends here—old and new. I have my three boys home for the first time in I don't know how many years, all thanks to my almost daughter."

A lump formed in Grace's throat. She'd grown to love Jean and Johnny. They were good people, and they'd welcomed her into their family in a way she'd been searching for all her life. She sniffed. "Oscar did all the organizing."

Jean put a hand on her arm. "Maybe, but only because of you. You've made him understand just how important family is. In wanting to share it with you, he's come to appreciate the value of a loving family, and now he's drawing ours back together. We've always been close, but we were drifting. None of us made the effort to get together. That's changing, and it makes me so happy."

Grace nodded. It made her happy, too. She smiled as Johnny came to join them and slid his arm around his wife's waist. Grace loved seeing them kiss and the way Jean rested her head against his shoulder—just like she did with Oscar.

"This is a great party; thank you, ladies."

Grace smiled at him. It was hard to believe that this man, this renowned, very wealthy doctor was thanking her for a party. She caught herself thinking it and stopped. She should believe it. She did believe it. He wasn't just some fancy doctor. He was Oscar's dad, and he was a wonderful human being whom she was happy to know.

"Something wrong?" asked Johnny.

She shook her head. "No. Everything's right. I'm glad you love your party, and I'm glad to be a part of it."

"Were you judging us again?" asked Jean with a knowing smile.

Grace nodded. Jean had been helping her work on that. Oscar had been right. His parents didn't judge people by their circumstances, but by their character. She was trying to learn to do the same.

Johnny smiled at her. "You're going to have to stop doing that when—"

Jean dug him in the ribs. He looked mortified and then they both smiled.

What was that about? She didn't get chance to find out as Oscar came to join them. He gave his parents a look she didn't understand. She got the impression they were hiding something, but she didn't know what. She looked around. Maybe she'd messed something up, and they were being polite about not telling her. Everything seemed okay. There was plenty of food and drink, and people were enjoying themselves. Though, on second thoughts, it seemed people were no longer talking and milling around. In fact, most of them were looking up at the deck where she was standing.

She turned to look at Oscar. There was something going on. He brought his hand up to his face, but his thumb couldn't hide the smirk underneath it.

She raised an eyebrow. "What I am missing?"

He grinned. "I'm not sure I'm ready to tell you yet."

She turned to his parents. They obviously knew something. They smiled at her. Jean looked as though she was fit to burst. Most conversations had stopped. She saw Hope smiling at her encouragingly. Then she spotted TJ and Chance carrying Terry and his wheelchair up the steps to join them. Louise was standing close to Reid, her arm linked through his while he looked slightly uncomfortable.

Grace pursed her lips and turned back to Oscar. "What's going on?"

He looked over at Terry and Spider who both nodded before turning back to her. "Okay, now I'm ready to tell you."

Grace's hand flew up to cover her mouth as he went down on one knee before her. "Grace Evans, I told you when I met you that you are one unusual lady, and I was right. You're special. I love you, I love everything about you. I love what you do for the people in your life, and most of all I love what you've done for me. I love who you are, and I love who I've become through knowing you. We're building a great life together, but I want more. I want to know that we're going to spend the rest of our lives together. Grace, will you marry me?"

Her heart was pounding in her ears as he held up a ring. It was the biggest diamond she'd ever seen. She looked at it and then looked into his eyes and he winked; the arrogant prick actually winked. "I'll get you a smaller one if you insist."

She laughed. She had to. That was Oscar. That was the man she loved, and for better or worse, she knew she'd love him for the rest of her life. "Yes," she breathed. "Yes, I will marry you."

He slid the ring onto her finger and got to his feet. He closed his arms around her, and she buried her face in his chest. That warm feeling, the intimacy they shared, the happiness in her heart filled her up and overflowed. It came out as tears— happy tears—and they flowed down her face as he lifted her chin and she kissed him. She had to be the happiest woman alive.

She got lost in a sea of hugs and well-wishes. His parents, his brothers, Hope, even his uncle, they all hugged her and welcomed her to the family—she was a part of a family! And she loved it. Louise bounced around her and demanded to be maid of honor. Spider wrapped her in a very rare hug. He didn't have many words, but the two of them didn't really need words. He was so happy for her, and she knew it. Terry held his arms up to her, and she sat down in his lap and for a moment they just stared at each other, each with tears streaming down past big smiles.

Oscar patted Terry on his back as Grace got up, and to her surprise, he squatted down beside Terry's chair and hugged him. "Thank you."

A fresh wave of tears came as she watched the two men embrace. She knew Oscar would always be grateful to him.

Jean and Louise were going around making sure everyone had a drink for a toast. Louise's tray was almost empty by the time she reached Terry. "Do you want something?" she asked. "I've got lemonade or…"

Terry laughed and tugged Grace's hand. "I don't want no lemonade. Me and Gracie, we're holding out for champagne and strawberries, right?"

Grace laughed with him. "Yes, we are, Terry. We certainly are."

Oscar gave her a puzzled look. He passed her and Terry a glass of champagne each. "There are strawberries inside. I can go get you some if that's what you want."

She shook her head and hugged him tightly. "You've already given me everything I could want and more."

He smiled down at her and dropped a kiss on the end of her nose. "We're only just getting started Mrs. Davenport."

As the tears filled her eyes again, she knew it was true. This was just the beginning, and she couldn't wait to live the rest of her life with him;

A Note from SJ

I hope you enjoyed getting to know the Davenports. Please let your friends know about the books if you feel they would enjoy them as well. It would be wonderful if you would leave me a review; I'd very much appreciate it.

There are so many more stories still to tell. The next book I'm working on is Mary Ellen and Antonio's story which will be out soon. TJ is in a hurry too and I plan to write his book, Marco, the final Hamiltons story and then the third Davenport brother, Reid, just as fast as my little fingers can type. Plus, there are more stories set at the Lake; the pilots want a Summer Lake Flyers series. And there is a bunch of cowboys who are all getting impatient for me to return to Montana. My plan at the moment is to finish with the Davenports and Hamiltons and then get to the next three series—Summer Lake Flyers, the new cowboys, who haven't told me what their series is called yet and the country singers in Nashville, beginning with Autumn and Matt. The older couples are growing impatient and I've still yet to figure out whether they'll end up as a series or as novellas when they get too impatient to wait any longer! The short version is that there are still a lot of stories to come.

In the meantime, be sure to check out my Remington Ranch series, if you haven't already.. You can get started with book one, Mason, which you can download in ebook form FREE from all the major online retailers but they are all available in paperback if you prefer.

If you'd like to keep in touch, there are a few options to keep up with me and my imaginary friends:

The best way is to Join up on the website for my Newsletter. Don't worry I won't bombard you! I'll let you know about upcoming releases, share a sneak peek or two and keep you in the loop for a couple of fun giveaways I have coming up :0)

You can join my readers group to chat about the books on Facebook or just browse and like my Facebook Page.

I occasionally attempt to say something in 140 characters or less(!) on Twitter

And I'm always in the process of updating my website at

www.sjmccoy.com

with new book updates and even some videos. Plus, you'll find the latest news on new releases and giveaways in my blog.

I love to hear from readers, so feel free to email me at AuthorSJMcCoy@gmail.com.. I'm better at that! :0)

I hope our paths will cross again soon. Until then, take care, and thanks for your support—you are the reason I write!

Love

SJ

PS Project Semicolon

You may have noticed that the final sentence of the story closed with a semi-colon. It isn't a typo. Project Semi Colon is a non-profit movement dedicated to presenting hope and love to those who are struggling with depression, suicide, addiction and self-injury. Project Semicolon exists to encourage, love and inspire. It's a movement I support with all my heart.

"A semicolon represents a sentence the author could have ended, but chose not to. The sentence is your life and the author is you."

\- Project Semicolon

This author started writing after her son was killed in a car crash. At the time I wanted my own story to be over, instead I chose to honour a promise to my son to write my 'silly stories' someday. I chose to escape into my fictional world. I know for many who struggle with depression, suicide can appear to be the only escape. The semicolon has become a symbol of support, and hopefully a reminder – Your story isn't over yet

Also by SJ McCoy

The Davenports
Oscar
Coming next
TJ

The Hamiltons
Cameron and Piper in Red wine and Roses
Chelsea and Grant in Champagne and Daisies
Coming Next
Mary Ellen and Antonio

Summer Lake Series
Love Like You've Never Been Hurt (FREE in ebook form)
Work Like You Don't Need the Money
Dance Like Nobody's Watching
Fly Like You've Never Been Grounded
Laugh Like You've Never Cried
Sing Like Nobody's Listening
Smile Like You Mean It
The Wedding Dance
Chasing Tomorrow
Dream Like Nothing's Impossible
Ride Like You've Never Fallen
Live Like There's No Tomorrow
The Wedding Flight

Remington Ranch Series
Mason (FREE in ebook form) and also available as Audio

Shane

Carter

Beau

Four Weddings and a Vendetta

A Chance and a Hope

Chance is a guy with a whole lot of story to tell. He's part of the fabric of both Summer Lake and Remington Ranch. He needed three whole books to tell his own story.

Chance Encounter

Finding Hope

Give Hope a Chance

About the Author

I'm SJ, a coffee addict, lover of chocolate and drinker of good red wines. I'm a lost soul and a hopeless romantic. Reading and writing are necessary parts of who I am. Though perhaps not as necessary as coffee! I can drink coffee without writing, but I can't write without coffee.

I grew up loving romance novels, my first boyfriends were book boyfriends, but life intervened, as it tends to do, and I wandered down the paths of non-fiction for many years. My life changed completely a few years ago and I returned to Romance to find my escape.

I write 'Sweet n Steamy' stories because to me there is enough angst and darkness in real life. My favorite romances are happy escapes with a focus on fun, friendships and happily-ever-afters, just like the ones I write.

These days I live in beautiful Montana, the last best place. If I'm not reading or writing, you'll find me just down the road in the park - Yellowstone. I have deer, eagles and the occasional bear for company, and I like it that way :0)